Augusta Joyce Crocheron

Representative Women of Deseret

A book of biographical sketches to accompany the picture bearing the

same title

Augusta Joyce Crocheron

Representative Women of Deseret
A book of biographical sketches to accompany the picture bearing the same title

ISBN/EAN: 9783337097530

Printed in Europe, USA, Canada, Australia, Japan

Cover: Foto ©Raphael Reischuk / pixelio.de

More available books at **www.hansebooks.com**

REPRESENTATIVE
WOMEN OF DESERET,

A BOOK OF

⇥BIOGRAPHICAL SKETCHES,⇤

To Accompany the PICTURE Bearing the Same Title.

COMPILED AND WRITTEN BY

AUGUSTA JOYCE CROCHERON,

Author of "WILD FLOWERS OF DESERET."

AND DEDICATED TO

*The originals of this Picture and Book, their co-laborers in the
Church, and every true heart that will receive
their testimonies.*

O, Spirits dear! Ye light the path
That else were lone and dim;
I follow where your sainted feet
Lead onward, up to Him,
And hear above life's discords, still,—
Your heav'n inspired hymn.

SALT LAKE CITY:
PRINTED BY J. C. GRAHAM & CO.
1884.

In presenting this picture, REPRESENTATIVE WOMEN OF DES-
ERET, before the public, an explanation may be appropriate
that the object may be rightly understood. The picture is intended to represent the Latter Day Saints Women's Organizations rather than to draw attention to those intellectual gifts
and acquirements which in this connection are but secondary
to the spiritual or missionary labors of those represented. As
in Salt Lake City is the head of these organizations, so these
spiritual laborers were selected by the precedence they hold.

Throughout our Territory, indeed beyond, are many as sincere and faithful, noble women, well deserving of every honor
contained herein, but there is of necessity a limit in the present work and that which would have been a pleasure to the
author became an impossibility at this time, but it is the purpose in due season to present another work which will be of
interest to our people.

It is not the purpose of the compiler of these sketches to
present a complete history of the subjects of the picture, to
which this book is merely an accompaniment to acquaint the
many who are strangers to them with their labors and their
virtues, to show as it were, what manner of people these
"Mormons" are. To do full justice to the originals would
require more space and ability than are mine. But if the eyes
of the stranger may thereby be opened to a knowledge of their
purity, integrity and faith in God, their heroic firmness and
the trials they have endured without wavering in allegiance
to their cause ; if any may be convinced that this people are
in earnest and in the right, and that God is with them ; if they

can realize that for men, Mormonism is not a cloak, a subterfuge and a selfish system; that our women are not from the dregs of civilization, led and controlled by stronger minds without a knowledge within themselves for their course, it will prove a joy and delight, a sweet return for my humble but earnest efforts. O, that these truthful testimonies falling upon hearts that are as blocks of ice toward us, might, like burning bullets melt their way therein, until, like Joseph's brethren, they should weep for injuries these have borne!

And to the young of our people, if this work shall cause them to appreciate their honored parents more by the nobility they have proven; if it shall cause them to weigh the object for which these sacrifices were endured against the poor temptations of the present time; if they shall question themselves, shall my parent's sacrifices count for naught? shall their example and their labors be lost on me? their hopes meet disappointment? If that command, " honor thy father and thy mother " shall prevail, and the sweet testimony of the Holy Spirit convince and strengthen them in the same service and faith unto their God, still sweeter and richer shall be the reward.

That this work may go forth from my humble home as a missionary, a silent worker of great good is my fervent hope.

A. J. C.

PREFACE.

In presenting the picture and book, REPRESENTATIVE WOMEN OF DESERET, to the public, I desire to first express my thanks to the ladies of the picture for their kindness and confidence. I thank Sister Eliza R. Snow Smith for her approval and sanction; Sister Emmeline B. Wells for her steadfast encouragement, and Bishop Hiram B. Clawson for his kind interest and advice. Published, as it has been, in part by subscription, I thank also my generous patrons.

Through a disappointment, so many embarrassments occurred that at one time I felt that no inducement, however beautiful, could again tempt me to so great (in my circumstances) an undertaking; but for me the Lord in His goodness opened the way; and towards James R. Miller, Dr. A. Farr and Zina D. H. Young, each, my heart thus expresses itself:

As Hagar in her lone despair
  Gazed hopeless o'er the desert drear,
Nor saw until her steps were led,
  The living waters, sweet and clear;
So I who strove through tedious days
  'Mid hopes that fled and fears that frowned—
Turned at thy name, and in thy heart,
  The boon I sought so long was found.

Not hers alone the story old—
  The earth is thronged with hearts distressed
That little dream how close beside
  The angel walks—to save and bless.

In compiling the brief sketches of Eliza R. Snow Smith, Zina D. H. Young, M. I. Horne and Prescendia L. Kimball,

I am indebted to the editor of the *Woman's Exponent*, their biographer. Several autobigraphies follow, and looking it all over, the thought rises—*how little I have done after all!* I have scarcely more than furnished the thread on which their gems were strung. Often I have paused, sorrowful that this work must be so brief: so much remains to be told. I have had sincerest joy in this labor, and if my efforts should be regarded as conferring any honor upon these ladies, it has been a greater honor to me to be accorded the privilege of tendering it, and of enjoying their acquaintance and friendship.

In conclusion, I would again refer to our First Lady, E. R. S. Smith; in a short time will appear her latest and largest book, an autobiography and history with genealogical record of her family, and dedicated to her noble brother, Apostle Lorenzo Snow. On her eightieth birthday, January 21, 1884, Sister Eliza was the recipient of a large surprise party given in honor of the day, in appreciation, love and respect of herself and labors, in the Social Hall, a building of histrionic association in the annals of Salt Lake City. It is wonderful indeed to contemplate the still youthful spirit, energy and ability of this lady; ever serene, gentle, forbearing with others; so carefully hiding her own weariness and leaving unmentioned whatever might trouble her; that the idea would never suggest itself to those not *intimately* associated with her, that she has anything to do but preside, receive and enjoy the loving expressions from her friends.

Hoping this volume may entertain and benefit the reader, and that all errors in *book-making* may be graciously pardoned, I will subscribe myself, dear public—

Your Servant and Friend,

AUGUSTA JOYCE CROCHERON.

INDEX.

ELIZA R. SNOW SMITH,

PRESIDENT OF THE WOMEN'S ORGANIZATIONS OF THE CHURCH OF JESUS CHRIST OF LATTER DAY SAINTS.

"Eliza R. Snow was born in Becket, Berkshire Co., Mass. Her parents were Oliver Snow of Mass., and Rosetta L. Pettibone, of Conn. They were of English descent, their parents having emigrated to America at an early period. In 1806, the family removed to Mantua, Portage Co., Ohio." Mr. and Mrs. Snow bestowed great care upon the education of their daughter, intellectual and domestic. She began her literary labors when quite young, her contributions over a *nom de plume* receiving much admiration.

Her grandfather was a revolutionary soldier, and his reminiscences created impressions upon her youthful mind that became part of her nature, developing into an intense national devotion.

"Two volumes of her 'Religious, Historical, Political' poems have been published, the First in Liverpool, England, in 1856, the Second in Salt Lake City." Her poems are life like and embody most of our Church history. To select her best poems would make a volume. The one by which she is best known, perhaps, is, "O, My Father, thou that dwellest," and ranks in its individuality and popularity as a Latter Day Saints' doctrinal hymn, with "The Spirit of God like a fire is burning." It is safe to say that these two hymns have wielded an influence beyond our power to estimate, in conveying the spirit of the Gospel to the hearts of the hearers. I have witnessed throngs of people standing outside a "Mormon" place of worship, listening to the singing forgetful for the time of their own personal affairs. They have fixed themselves upon the memory of all who ever heard them. "O My Father" contains doctrine that was new to the world, it was the essence of Mormonism. Every Mormon child is familiar with it and would recognize it in any country. It has been sung to many tunes,

several have been composed for it. Of these, I once heard
Pres. Brigham Young, in the St. George Temple, designate
his preference thus: "Will the Parowan choir please sing
'O My Father,' to that sweet, gentle air I love so well?"
The air was "Gentle Annie," a strange choice it sounded, but
the effect proved the correctness of his taste.

"Sister Eliza early devoted her attention to the Scriptures
and in her girlhood formed the acquaintance of the famous
preacher and scholar, Alexander Campbell, and other noted
divines. In 1835, she went to Kirtland, Ohio, and boarded in
the family of the Prophet Joseph, teaching a select school for
young ladies. Miss Snow returned home to visit her parents
but on the 1st of January, 1837, bade farewell to her paternal
home, to share the joys or the afflictions of the Latter Day
Saints.

"She became a governess to the children of the Prophet,
and was a companion for Emma, his wife, for a number of
years.

"From means she brought with her, Miss Snow gave freely
toward building the Kirtland Temple. Persecution soon arose
and raged so that, with her family who had now joined the
Church, she left Kirtland, going to Davies Co., Mo. On the
10th of December, 1838, Miss Snow with her father's family,
left Davies Co., the Mormons in that locality having been
ordered by the Governor to leave the county within ten days.

"They passed through almost unendurable sufferings, and
reaching Far West found the Prophet and many others had
been dragged to jail leaving their families destitute. March
1839, they left Far West leaving much of their property behind.
Eliza and her sister stopped in Quincy, Ill., awhile. In July
1839, Miss Snow went to Commerce, (since called Nauvoo) to
teach school. During her seven years' residence there she
wrote much and advanced rapidly in her knowledge of the
principles of the Gospel. Here, the Relief Society was organized by Joseph, March, 1842, and Sister Eliza was chosen for
secretary." There are now three hundred branches of the
Relief Society. "Eliza was at this time the wife of the
Prophet. In the latter part of July 1842, Mrs. Smith, Presi-

dent of the Relief Society, proposed a petition to Governor
Carlin, asking his protection of Joseph. Sister Eliza, as
secretary, wrote the petition which was signed by several
hundred ladies, and in company with President Emma and
Mrs. Warren Smith visited the Governor at his residence in
Quincy, Adams Co., Ill., where they were most cordially
received by the Governor. He replied to them, 'I believe
Mr. Smith is innocent.' Soon after their return home they
learned that the Governor in connection with Missouri officials
was plotting the destruction of the lives of those noble men.

"The Prophet and Patriarch were massacred! For awhile,
thought of all else was forgotten but this overwhelming woe.
But God gave them his sustaining love, and Eliza, widowed,
turned again to the work Joseph had established, consecrating
even her life to its service. The Temple was at length finished,
and Sister Eliza then began another era, ministering in the
Temple in the holy rites that pertain to the House of the Lord,
as Priestess and Mother in Israel to hundreds of her sex.

"In Feb., 1846, she left Nauvoo, on her way to the Rocky
Mountains. At the middle Fork of Green River they stopped
at one of the resting places. Here Sister Eliza and friends
with whom the latter traveled, lived in a log house laid up
like children's cob houses, with cracks from one to four inches
wide. A tent cloth stretched over the top, blankets and
carpets hung up inside as protection against the inclement
weather. On the 19th of August when they were leaving here,
they were minus a teamster. Sister Eliza undertook to drive
ox team, and after some experience became an adept. August
27th they crossed the Missouri river, and on the 28th, arrived
at Winter Quarters. From constant exposure and continued
hardships Sister Eliza broke down. Fever set in, chills and
fever followed; heavy rains came on and she was wet nearly
from head to foot. She felt that she stood at the gates of
death, it was but a step beyond, and once inside the portals
she would be free from pain and suffering. But the great life-
work lay before her, and she summoned courage and supreme
faith to her aid. They moved into a log house partly
finished, no chinking, no chimney. The fire was built on one

side, and the room which had no floor was always filled with smoke. The cooking had to be done out of doors, the intense cold being preferable to the smoke." About the close of the year she received the sad news of the death of her mother.

"April 7th, 1847, the pioneers under the direction of President Brigham Young started to find a gathering place for the Pilgrim Saints. In June Sister Eliza resumed her journey westward. Nursing the sick in tents and wagons, and burying the dead by the wayside in the wild desert were indeed mournful, yes, pitiful. On the 4th of August, several of the Mormon Batallion returning to Winter Quarters, met the Pilgrim Companies, and joyful indeed was the meeting for they were husbands, fathers, brothers and sons of women who were in those companies. They soon met the returning pioneers and heard of the resting place found, and arrived safely in the valley in October. Here Sister Eliza took up her abode with Mrs. Clara Decker Young. Shortly after, the Saints numbering six hundred arrived in the valley, a pole was erected and the *flag* which had been preserved with the greatest care, was raised. * * As time passed on a place was selected and consecrated in which holy ordinances might be administered. Sister Eliza was called upon to take part, in which calling she has officiated up to the present. When the wards and settlements were pretty generally systematized, Pres. Young re-organized the Relief Society. He called on Sister Eliza to assist, and associate with her in the labor, Zina D. Young; this gave to them the precedence which they have since held.

"At a Mass Meeting held in this city January 13th, 1870, in the Old Tabernacle, (where the Assembly Hall now stands) by about 6,000 women to protest against the 'Cullom Bill,' Sister Eliza made a strong and brilliant speech. Politically this was the turning point in the history of the women of Utah. A few weeks later and the women of Utah received the right of franchise. They will ever hold Governor S. A. Mann in special grateful remembrance. * * In 1854-5, the Lion House was completed and Sister Eliza has ever since resided there. It was some years later before the domestic spinning, dyeing and weaving were discontinued, in these things Sister Eliza also excelled.

"In 1869, the Retrenchment Meetings were by the counsel of Pres. Young, organized. An association with a presiding board of seven officers. These meetings are still held in the Fourteenth Ward Assembly Rooms semi-monthly, at the same hour, the same ladies presiding, excepting Sister M. T. Smoot since removed to Provo. Here good instructions are given, and here the Junior Associations' secretaries bring the minutes of their respective Wards' Meetings, also the secretaries of the Primary Associations, (girls under twelve years of age, generally,) thus bringing together for mutual benefit an interchange of ideas, experience and suggestions, the aged veterans, the younger matrons and maidens, and little children.

"October 26th, 1872, Sister Eliza left Salt Lake City on a journey to the Holy Land, her brother, Apostle Lorenzo Snow, joining her in Ogden. Pres. George A. Smith and party met them in New York. They took the steamer for Liverpool November 5th. In Rome Sister Eliza spent five days, visited Naples, Corfu, Alexandria, Cairo, Suez, Joppa, the plains of Sharon, the Valley of Ajelon became realized, and in due time they beheld Jerusalem. This tour through the Holy Land was a mission pertaining to the Latter Day Work. An account of the trip was published in book form, entitled 'Palestine Tourists.' Sunday, March 2nd, 1873, they ascended the Mount of Olives, and held service there after the manner of the Holy Priesthood as revealed in this dispensation. March 25th, embarked for Constantinople. Sister Eliza had been enduring twenty-nine days of tent life, and twenty-one of riding on horseback. And this in her seventieth year! At Athens they took tea with the American Minister, and met the American Consul General to Constantinople. They visited Munich then went to Vienna and thence to Hamburg. May 16th, 1873, they took steamer for London, and met the Saints in their Conference, May 25th. Embarked for home on the 28th. Returning early in July, she visited many old scenes and friends of her early life, received with honors from place to place. So quiet was her return to Utah, that four days elapsed

before her many friends became aware of it. A brief rest
sufficed, Sister Eliza could not be idle. She visited Ogden
and Provo in August, Cache Valley in September, holding
meetings in these and many other places.

"Just after the October Conference of 1876, Sister Eliza
entered upon the superintendency of the 'Woman's Store,' a
Commission House for Utah home made goods. Officers and
employees were women. During this year she prepared her
second volume of poems for the press, also assisted in selecting
and preparing the manuscript for the 'Women of Mormondom,' and in raising funds for its publication, and not least of
all, gave the proof her attention. Also still continued her
labors in the House of the Lord." At this time occurred the
death of President Brigham Young. To one so disciplined in
order, with such continuity of purpose, such adhesiveness to
principle and friends, it would seem that to ordinary persons,
the loss of one in whose house she had her place, and whose
friendship and counsels she had shared for over twenty-five
years, would be an overwhelming shock. But the same
strength of mind which had risen from the martyrdom of the
Prophet and Patriarch supported her again, and she "renewed
her diligence, if it were possible, in her broad field of labor."
Political events and duties occupied her attention during December and January 1878. During the ensuing summer she
traveled hundreds of miles, holding generally two meetings a
day wherever they stopped. While attending a meeting at
Farmington, Davis Co., the efforts of Sister Aurelia, Spencer,
Rogers received her consideration and the Primary Associations, for children, became part of our system. "The first
Organization at Farmington dates from September 7th, 1878;
about this time an Association was organized in the Eleventh
Ward of this city, taking the lead." This new feature so suggestive of great benefit to the children so enlisted her feelings
that she has visited most of the settlements and wards in this
matter organizing Associations. Sister Eliza returned from a
long tour of missionary labor just in time to preside at a grand
Mass Meeting of 15,000 women, held in the Theatre, November
16th, 1878, in reply to to representations of the Anti-Polygam-

ic Society. The year 1880 was spent visiting the L. D. S. Women's Organizations, and the production of the Childrens Primary Hymn Book, soon followed by a tune book to accompany the above. On Saturday, July 17th, Fourteenth Ward Assembly Rooms, President John Taylor ordained Sister Eliza to the office to which she had been elected; President of Latter Day Saints' Women's Organizations throughout the world, wherever our people are; also, Sister Zina D. H. Young as her First Counselor, Elizabeth A. Whitney (since deceased) Second Counselor, Sarah M. Kimball as Secretary, and Mary Isabella Horne as Treasurer.

"In August Sister Eliza visited Sanpete Co., and in Thistle Valley assisted the Bishop in organizing a Relief Society, with an Indian sister as a counselor; the first Indian woman ordained and set apart to an office in this dispensation. November 8th, Sister Eliza accompanied by Sister Zina D. Young, left home for St. George to do a work in the Temple. They traveled over one thousand miles in carriages and wagons, doing missionary work among the Saints. In St. George the anniversary of Sister Eliza's birthday was publicly celebrated, and on the same day the people of Weber Stake paid a delicate tribute to the honorable lady by a similar celebration at Ogden City.

"Sisters Eliza and Zina returned from St. George March 31st, and were met at the depot by a party of thirty ladies who escorted them to the Lion House, where a reception, a welcome home, awaited them. In 1881, during the intervals of her many public duties, she prepared her new book Bible Questions and Answers. In September, visited Thistle Valley, organizing a Primary Association with ten little Indian children enrolled as members. April 1883, the Relief Society was organized among the Indians at Washakie, an Indian village in Box Elder Co. After duly considering the long-felt necessity among our own people of an institution for the sick and injured, where the ordinances of faith might be administered freely and without restraint, in fact, one that we might term our own, and as one of the links in our system of organizations, the sisters took a course that led to the establishment of the Deseret Hospital, at which institution the dedication services were held, July 17th, 1882, by the First Presidency, Stake Presidency, Apostles Wilford Woodruff and F. D. Richards; Mayor William Jennings, C. W. Penrose, Editor *Deseret News*, L. John Nuttall and Joseph Horne being present. Eliza R. S. Smith, President, E. B. Wells, Secretary."

I will conclude this brief sketch with one of her latest poems:

BURY ME QUIETLY WHEN I DIE.

When my spirit ascends to the world above,
To smile with the choirs in celestial love,
Let the finger of silence control the bell,
To restrain the chime of a funeral knell,
Let no mourning strain—not a sound be heard,
By which a pulse of the heart is stirred—
No note of sorrow to prompt a sigh;
Bury me quietly when I die.

I am aiming to earn a celestial crown—
To merit a heavenly; pure renown;
And, whether in grave or in tomb I'm laid,
Beneath the tall oak or the cypress shade;
Whether at home with dear friends around;
Or in distant lands upon stranger ground—
Under wintry clouds or a summer sky;
Bury me quietly when I die.

What avail the parade and the splendor here,
To a legal heir to a heavenly sphere?
To the heirs of salvation what is the worth,
In their perishing state, the frail things of earth?
What is death to the good, but an entrance gate
That is placed on the verge of a rich estate
Where commissioned escorts are waiting by?
Bury me quietly when I die.

On the "iron rod" I have laid my hold;
If I keep the faith, and like Paul of old
Shall have "fought the good fight" and Christ the Lord
Has a crown in store with a full reward
Of the holy priesthood in fulness rife,
With the gifts and the powers of an endless life,

And a glorious mansion for me on high;
Bury me quietly when I die.

*   *   *   *   *   *   *   *   *   *   *   *   *   *   *   *

Like a beacon that rises o'er ocean's wave,
There's a light—there's a life beyond the grave;
The future is bright and it beckons me on
Where the noble and pure and the brave have gone;
Those who have battled for truth with their mind and might,
With their garments clean and their armor bright;
They are dwelling with God in a world on high:
Bury me quietly when I die.

ZINA D. H. YOUNG,

FIRST COUNSELOR TO THE PRESIDENT OF THE L. D. S. WOMEN'S
ORGANIZATIONS.

"And he shall turn the hearts of the fathers to the children, and the hearts of the children to their fathers, lest I come and smite the earth with a curse." How fitting are these sacred words to the subject of this sketch and her family. In obedience to this command renewed in this dispensation, searching through their genealogical records for ten generations back, they have brought forth to light, and to eternal life in the celestial kingdom of God, the forgotten and unknown ancestry of their family, finding now and then some noble representative of their race linked with even a kingdom's honor, and at last, far back, upon the throne of England.

Sister Zina's career of religious devotion and service is not a new feature in the Huntington family, nor America a new field of labor to them. One hundred years ago Lady Salina Huntington, saving to herself only sufficient for the real needs of life, devoted a great portion of her vast fortune to missionary service, for the introduction of Christianity among the North American Indians, by the founding of schools for the natives and the support of ministers and teachers. "She allowed herself but one dress a year. Lady Salina Huntington was the second daughter of the Earl of Ferrars. She was born in 1707, and was the co-laborer of Whitefield and Wesley. 'The pedigree of Lady Huntington and her husband, and of George Washington, first President of the United States, (as traced by Mapleson in his researches) meet in the same parentage.' 'Lady Huntington and her chaplains often journeyed during the summer, making their presence a means of religious revivals wherever they went. A church needed. With her, to resolve was to accomplish. Her jewels she determined to offer to the Lord. They were sold for six hundred and ninety-eight pounds, and with this she erected a house of worship in 1760. Her daughter, Lady Salina, was one of the six earls daughters chosen to assist the Princess Augusta to bear the train of Queen Charlotte on her coronatiion day." Did it foreshadow an era of revelations dawning upon the world, when she prayed "that God would give us new bread, not stale, but what was baked in the oven that day." Lady Huntington built seven chapels, her private property, beside aiding sixty others. At the age of eighty-four a few hours before the last struggle she whispered joyfully, "I shall go to my Father to-night," and so she went home, June 17th, 1791.

Thus by birthright and by heritage is the land of Freedom the Huntingtons field of religious labor. The mantles of Lady Huntington and remoter noble ancestors have at last been lifted from the silence and the shadows of departed centuries to the shoulders of worthy descendants and representatives, who are doing works of greater magnitude than they ever comprehended. Superintended by Dimock B. Huntington, and assisted by the family, Zina and her sister Prescinda have been baptized for ten generations, numbering nearly five thousand.

By permission I select from matter collected and published by Emmeline B. Wells, in *Woman's Exponent* the following portions of biography:

"Zina Diantha Huntington was born January 31st, 1821, at Watertown. Her father was William Huntington, her mother Zina Baker, whose father was one of the first physicians in New Hampshire. Her grandmother on the mother's side was Dorcas Dimock, 'descended from the noble family of Dimocks, whose representatives held the hereditary knight-championship of England; instance: Sir Edward Dymock, Queen Elizabeth's champion.'

"The father of Mrs. Zina D. H. Young was also a patriot and served in the war of 1812. Samuel Huntington, one of the signers of the Declaration of Independence, was the uncle of this old revolutionary soldier. She says: 'My fathers family is directly descended from Simon Huntington, the Puritan immigrant who sailed for America in 1633. He died at sea, but left three sons and his widow, Margaret. The church records of Roxbury, Mass., contain the earliest record of the Huntington name known in New England, and is in the hand-writing of the Rev. John Elliot himself, the pastor of that ancient church. This is the record: 'Margaret Huntington, widow, came in 1633, her husband died by the way of small pox. She brought children with her.' 'My grandfather, Wm. Huntington, the revolutionary soldier, married Prescinda Lathrop, and was one of the first settlers in the Black River Valley, Northern New York. The Huntingtons and Lathrops intermarried, and my sister Prescinda Lathrop Huntington, bears the family name of generations. The Huntingtons embraced the Gospel at Watertown, New York, and Zina D., when only fifteen years old was baptized by the Patriarch Hyrum Smith, August 14th, 1835, and soon after went to Kirtland with her father's family. In this year she received the gift of tongues. On one occasion in the Kirtland Temple she heard a whole invisible choir of angels singing, till the house seemed filled with numberless voices. At Kirkland she received the gift of interpretation. She was also at the memorable Pentecost when the spirit of God filled the house like a mighty, rushing wind. Zina was also a member of the Kirtland Temple Choir, of whom but few are now living.

Sister Zina experienced the persecutions in Missouri, during which the mother died from fatigue and privation, and only two of their family were able to follow her remains to their resting place. She says; "Thus died my martyred mother."

Sister Zina was married in Nauvoo, and had two sons, but this not proving a happy union, she subsequently separated from her husband. Joseph Smith taught her the principle of marriage for eternity, and she accepted it as a divine revelation, and was sealed to the Prophet for time and eternity, after the order of the new and everlasting Covenant.

Sister Zina was a member of the first organization of the Relief Society at Nauvoo, and when the Temple was ready for the ordinances to be performed, received there her blessings and endowments. After the martyrdom of the Prophet Joseph and Hyrum, she was united in marriage for time to Brigham Young, and with the Saints left Nauvoo in the month of February, crossing the Mississippi on the ice. Arriving at Mt. Pisgah, a resting place for the exiles, Father Huntington was called to preside and Zina D., with her two little boys remained with him temporarily. Sickness visited the camp, and deaths were so frequent that help could not be obtained to make coffins. Many were buried with split logs at the bottom of the grave and brush at the sides, that being all that could be done by mourning friends. Her father was taken sick, in eighteen days he died. After these days of trial she went to Winter Quarters, and was welcomed into the family of Brigham Young. With them, she in May 1848, began the journey to this valley, walking, driving team, cooking beside camp-fires, and in September arrived here, living in tents and wagons until log houses could be built. Here, April 3rd, 1850, was born Zina, daughter of Brigham Young and Zina D. Young.

When the Relief Society was reorganized in Utah by President Brigham Young, Sister Zina was one of the first identified with that work, as Treasurer, and when Sister Eliza was called to preside over all the Relief Societies, she chose Zina as her Counselor.

One of the most useful fields of her labor, has been sericulture. She has raised cocoons, attending to them with her own hands, and had charge of a large cocoonery and mulberry orchard belonging to President Young. When the Silk Association was organized, June 15th, 1876, she was chosen President. Great good was accomplished, mulberry trees were planted and cocoons raised in every part of the Territory where the climate would permit. A good article of silk was manufactured with home machinery." Sister Zina also took a course of medical studies, being perhaps the first to adopt the wish of President Young, for as many of the sisters as would be useful for the practice in the many settlements, among their own sex; to qualify themselves. Ladies came from different settlements, stimulated by her example. "In all departments of woman's labor for the public good, Sister Zina had been found at her post doing her share of active work in the best manner possible. She has traveled among the different settlements visiting organized societies, or assisting Sister Eliza or the local authorities in organizing. "At a Mass Meeting of ladies held in this city, November 16th, 1878, Sister Zina delivered a very eloquent impromptu address." I was one of the reporters on that occasion, and noting the increasing earnestness in her voice and words, raised my eyes to her standing just before the table we were using. Suddenly, as though her words struck home like an electric shock, several gentlemen sitting at my right hand, clutching the arms of their chairs, started as though they would rise to their feet; their faces burning with the truths they heard, their eyes fixed upon her fearless face and uplifted hands. I can never forget that moment. It was more than eloquence, it was inspiration. I will quote that portion of her address.

"The principle of our religion that is assailed is one that lies deep in my heart. Could I ask the heavens to listen; could I beseech the earth to be still, and the brave men who possess the spirit of a Washington to hear what I am about to say. I am the daughter of a Master Mason! I am the widow of a Master Mason, who, when leaping from the window of Carthage Jail pierced with bullets, made the Masonic sign of distress; but, gentlemen, (addressing the representatives of the press that were present) those signs were not heeded except by the God of heaven. That man, the Prophet of the Almighty, was massacred without mercy! Sisters, this is the first time in my life that I have dared to give utterance to this fact, but I thought I could trust my soul to say it on this occasion; and I say it now in the fear of Israel's God, and I say it in the presence of these gentlemen and I wish my voice could be heard by the whole brotherhood of Masons through-out our proud land. That institution I honor. If its principles were practiced and strictly adhered to would there be a trespass upon virtue? No indeed. Would the honorable wife or daughter be intruded upon with impunity? Nay, verily. Would that the ladies of America, with the honorable Mrs. Hayes at their head; would that the Congress of the United States, the law makers of our nation, could produce a balm for the many evils which exist in our land through the abuse of virtue, or could so legislate that virtue could be protected and cherished as the life which heaven has given us. We in common with many women throughout our broad land would hail with joy the approach of such deliverance, for such is the deliverance that woman needs. The principle of plural marriage is honorable; it is a principle of the Gods, it is heaven born. God revealed it to us as a saving principle; we have accepted it as such, and we know it is of him for the fruits of it are holy. Even the Saviour, Himself, traces his lineage back to polygamic parents. We are proud of the principle because we know its true worth, and we want our children to practice it, that through us a race of men and women may grow up possessing sound minds in sound bodies, who shall live to the age of a tree." "During the summer of 1879, Sister Zina decided to take a trip to the Sandwich Islands for her health, and was accompanied by Miss Susa Young. She had the opportunity of meeting many persons of note to whom she imparted correct information regarding our people; distributing tracts and books. Great respect was paid her and many ovations. She assisted the native members of our church in getting an organ for their meetings, and contributed liberally for other benevolent purposes." "On her return she spent most of her time attending meetings of the various organizations. Sericulture was not forgotten or neglected. She also continued her labors in the House of the Lord. In the fall of 1880, Sisters Zina and Eliza went to St. George, to labor in the Temple, and visit the organizations of the women and children, wherever practicable. They held meetings by the way, often camped out over night, and traveled thus over one thousand miles. Returning March 31st, 1881, they were met at the depot by a party of thirty ladies, in carriages, who escorted them to the Lion House where a reception of welcome home awaited them.

August 20th, 1831, Sister Zina, accompanied by her foster son, Lieut. Willard Young, started for New York to gather up the records of her relatives. Dr. E. B. Ferguson was going to pursue her medical studies further in some branches, to be of greater service among the people. Previous to their going, they were blest and set apart by the First Presidency of the Church, to speak upon the principles of our faith if opportunity presented.

Sister Zina was cordially received by her relatives, and invited to speak in Sunday School and Temperance Meetings. Visited New York City, and listened to many celebrated divines. Attended the Woman's Congress at Buffalo, N. Y., but was refused five minutes to represent the women of Utah. Visited Watertown, N. Y., then to Vermont, and thence to Albany Co., and spoke in several meetings. Sister Zina returned to New York to attend the N. W. S. A. Convention, without opportunity of addressing them. She however assisted the brethren in organizing a Relief Society in New York. With Lieut. Willard Young she visited West Point. Mrs. Young returned to this city March 7th, received by her daughters and many friends, the return being the occasion for a most delightful party. On the Friday following, the Relief Society Conference convened, and her many friends had the opportunity of welcoming her home.

Picture and words are alike powerless to convey the beauty of her face, her spirit and her life. Each succeeding year adds a tenderer line to her face, a sweeter, gentler intonation to her voice, a more perceptible power to her spirit from the celestial fountains of faith; widens the circle of her friends, strengthens and deepens their love for her, and brings a richer harvest of noble labors to her name. Could I say more? I could not say less of her who has for eighteen years been my most intimate friend, my counselor, my second mother. A mother, not to me alone, to her belongs in its sweetest, widest sense, the name—a "mother in Israel."

MARY ISABELLA HORNE,

TREASURER OF THE PRESIDING BOARD OF THE L. D. S. WOMEN'S
ORGANIZATIONS.

"I was born November 20th, 1818, in the town of Rainshaw,
County of Kent, England. I am the daughter of Stephen and
Mary Ann Hales, and the eldest daughter of a large family.
My parents were honest, industrious people. I was taught
to pray when very young, to be honest and truthful, to be
kind to my associates, and to do good to all around us. My
early years were spent in attending school and in assisting my
mother in domestic duties."

"Mrs. Horne's father was a Methodist, and her mother a
member of the Church of England. Mrs. Horne as a child,
had very strong religious tendencies, and when requested by
her Sabbath School teacher to commit to memory two or
three verses from the Bible, she would learn a whole chapter
or perhaps two, and recite without being prompted.

"When only in her eleventh year, she became so fascinated
with the Bible that her leisure hours after the labors of the
day were over, were employed in reading and studying the
history and incidents, the sublime parables and teachings
contained in that sacred work; thus prepared to receive in
due time the Gospel of the new and last dispensation. In
1832, Mrs. Horne's parents decided to emigrate, and concluded
to go to upper Canada. April 6th, they left England with a
family of five sons and two daughters.

"One little boy died upon the way. On the 16th of June,
they arrived in York, strangers in a strange land, where the
cholera was making fearful ravages, but the Lord preserved
them all in health. The following spring, 1833, the family removed to the country, about eight miles from York. Mrs.

3

Hales' health was delicate and the care of the whole family devolved upon Mary Isabella, only fifteen years of age.

"In the spring of 1834, she attended a Methodist camp meeting in the neighborhoood, where she first met Mr. Joseph Horne, and two years afterward, Joseph Horne and Mary Isabella were united in marriage on the 9th of May, 1836."

Only about one month of their wedded life had passed when they heard a rumor that a man professing to be sent of God, to preach to the people would hold a meeting about a mile distant.

Mr. and Mrs. Horne attended this meeting and there they first heard the Gospel, proclaimed by Elder Orson Pratt, but little knew how the course of their life would be changed by receiving this great light. Mrs. Horne was baptized in July, 1836, by Elder Orson Hyde, and ever after her house was a home for the elders, and a place where meetings were held. In the latter part of the summer of 1837, she first saw the Prophet Joseph, also Sidney Rigdon and Thomas B. Marsh."

She says: "On shaking hands with the Prophet Joseph Smith, I received the holy spirit in such great abundance that I felt it thrill my whole system from the crown of my head to the soles of my feet. 1 had never beheld so lovely a countenance, nobility and goodness were in every feature. I said to myself, 'O Lord, I thank thee for granting the desire of my girlish heart in permitting me to associate with prophets and apostles.'" "In March 1838, while the weather was still wintry, Mr. and Mrs. Horne bade farewell to their home, and with a few saints started for the gathering-place of the people of God.

"At Huntsville, Mrs. Horne was introduced to Father and Mother Smith; Father Smith was the Patriarch of the church, and under his hands she received a patriarchal blessing. In August, with a babe less than a month old, they removed to Far West, and were obliged to go into a log house without doors or windows. It was about this time that the excitement in Missouri raged, and persecution was at its height. Mrs. Horne was alone much night and day, her husband being on guard. In the spring of 1839, Mrs. Horne and family left Missouri as exiles, and sought an asylum in Quincy, Ill., where for awhile they had peace. While in Quincy, Mrs. Horne was one of those favored ones who had the privilege of entertaining and waiting upon the Prophet Joseph and Hyrum, the Patriarch. In the month of March, Mr. and Mrs. Horne moved to Nauvoo by wagon, over the then wild prairies. They lived in a lumber shanty for eight months, and in November Mr. Horne moved his family into his own house, still unfinished. Here in 'Nauvoo the beautiful,' Mr. Horne through diligent labor at last succeeded in establishing a flourishing business and his family were looked upon by the Saints as quite well situated. On the 2nd of April, 1844, Mrs. Horne received a patriarchal blessing under the hands of Hyrum Smith, the patriarch of the Church." On the 27th of the June following, occurred the martyrdom of Joseph and Hyrum. Mrs. Horne says, "On the 28th day of June, I took my last look on earth of Joseph and Hyrum Smith! May I never experience another day similar to that. I do not wish to recall the scene." On the 9th of July was born her fifth son. In January, 1846, Mrs. Horne went into the Nauvoo Temple, receiving the ordinances of the House of the Lord, and assisted in administering to others. In February Mr. Horne closed his business and bade adieu to their home and camped with the Saints on Sugar Creek, Iowa.

In March moved on to Garden Grove, and then to Mt. Pisgah. Here, Mrs. Horne had born to her a daughter, born in a wagon. When the babe was three days old, Mrs. Horne started again on her way, arriving at Council Bluffs about the last of June, moving into a log cabin. Here she was so sick it was feared she would not recover. Elder Orson Pratt administered to her and prophesied she would do a good work in Israel. In June of the same year, she left with the first company across the plains that followed the pioneers to the valley of Salt Lake. That was indeed a remarkable journey and all those who traveled hither at that time deserve the title of pioneers. They opened the way and braved the perils of the desert and the experience of living in this sterile land. They ploughed and planted and fought against the fearful odds of crickets, grasshoppers and death. The company in which Mrs. Horne traveled, arrived here October 6th, 1847, and as soon as the Fort was completed she moved into it, and lived in a log cabin two years, enduring all the exigencies incident to the settling of a new Indian country, among which were living on short rations, a part of which was roots and thistles. On the 16th of January, 1849, another daughter was added to the family. As soon as possible after arriving in a new and destitute country, Mr. and Mrs. Horne made themselves a home in the Fourteenth Ward, which they still retain. "In speaking of her first knowledge of the order of celestial marriage, she says, she has had strong testimony for herself that it is of God. Mrs. Horne has borne herself nobly in all the different phases of plural domestic relations." Mrs. Horne was a member of the Relief Society in Nauvoo, and in the first organization of the Fourteenth Ward in this city, was a counselor to President Phoebe W. Woodruff.

In May, 1858, Mrs. Horne moved as far south as Parowan, her husband being called on a mission still further south, in "Dixie." Against every disadvantage, Mrs. Horne performed this journey of two hundred and fifty miles, this mother with her ten children, the youngest a babe of six months. In September their mission was fulfilled and Mrs. Horne returned home, Mr. Horne returning from his mission soon after. "December 12th, 1867, Mrs. Horne was chosen by Bishop A. Hoagland, of the Fourteenth Ward, to preside over the Relief Society in that ward. It was a great surprise to her, she was at that time very timid.

Under the wise management of the President, the society increased in numbers, great good was accomplished in the relief of the poor and afflicted, and means multiplied in the Treasury. A two story brick building has been erected by the society, part of which is rented for a store, and the upper story used for meetings. The society also own a good granary and a quantity of wheat. Mrs. Horne's success as a leader was so apparent and her course so consistent, President Young had such confidence in her, he gave her a very important mission among the sisters; this was called Retrenchment. In due time a meeting was held in the Fifteententh Ward Schoolhouse, and from there adjourned to the Fourteenth Ward Assembly Rooms, and from that time until the present, Mrs. Horne has presided at these regular semi-monthly meetings of the Ladies' General Retrenchment Associations. When President Young instructed Sister Eliza to go through the Territory and organize the young ladies into associations for mutual improvement, Mrs. Horne was called to assist. She has organized many of the Young Ladies Associations, also Primary Associations. At the time of the passage of the Cullom Bill in January, 1876, a grand Mass Meeting was called to convene in the Old Tabernacle, Salt Lake City. Mrs. Horne took an active part in the proceedings, being one of the committee to draft resolutions. In February following, the bill was passed, granting suffrage to the women of Utah. Mrs. Horne was one of a committee of ladies who waited upon Governor S. A. Mann to express the gratitude of Mormon women for his signing of the document. December 1877, Mrs. Horne was chosen to preside over the Relief Societies of this stake of Zion. She was elected a delegate from Salt Lake County, to the Territorial Convention held in this city, commencing October 9th, and was called upon to address them. Mrs. Horne was one of the committee appointed to wait upon the delegate nominated at the Convention, and inform him of the honor conferred upon him.

When Mrs. Horne was sixty years of age, upon the demise of her daughter-in-law, Mrs. Lydia Weiler Horne, she took the babe six weeks old to raise. This after rearing a family, and seeing each take honored places in the world.

Mrs. Horne has been an officer and worker in the silk industry from the beginning. At the organization of the board of officers for the Deseret Hospital, May 1882, Mrs. Horne was elected Chairman of the Executive Committee.

November 20th, 1882, was the forty-sixth anniversary of

Mr. and Mrs. Horne's wedding day. At the reception they held, an elegant photograph album was presented from lady friends, each of whom was to contribute her picture. Congratulations from children, Mayor Jennings and Judge Miner, with loving and sincere good wishes from all, for the future, made this a day long to be remembered. ''

I am indebted to the pen of Emmeline·B. Wells, editor of the "Woman's Exponent," for the points I have selected for this sketch, to whom the original referred me as possessing all I would wish to obtain. Perhaps, it would be no more than justice to the author, to quote also from the same source, the record her family have so far, made, thereby reflecting credit upon their noble parents. It will also give to the world the history in brief of *one* Mormon family, reared in the teachings, examples and associations of Mormonism, not omitting the system of celestial marriage.

'' By their fruits ye shall know them. ''

"Henry, the eldest son, was for eleven years Bishop in Paris, Idaho, in 1880, moved to Arizona, to assist in colonizing there.

"Joseph, when about twenty years of age, was called on a mission to Switzerland, where he obtained a thorough knowledge of the German language. Returned, and was for ten years Bishop of Gunnison, Sanpete Co., again called to Switzerland to preside over the Swiss and German missions and edit the *Stern*. In 1878, he was called to the Bishopric in Richfield, Sevier Co., is also mayor of that city.

"Richard is a teacher; was superintendent of Sunday-schools in Beaver, and has filled several home missions.

"John, the youngest son, was the first President of the Young Men's Mutual Improvement Association in the Fourteenth Ward. Her eldest daughter, Mrs. Elizabeth Webb, lives in Millard Co., a lady who might grace any society.

"Nora married George, son of Orson Spencer, somewhat famous in Church history for his valuable writings and great missionary work in America and Europe.

"Julia married Wm. Burton, and died one year after marriage, leaving a baby daughter. She was the first President of the Young Ladies Mutual Improvement Associaton of the Fourteenth Ward.

"Cornelia was later made the President. Miss Cornelia was also for three or four years business manager of the *Woman's Exponent*. She is the wife of James Clayton.

" Minnie, her twin sister, was for several years Secretary of the Young Ladies Mutual Improvement Association and the Sunday-school. Since her marriage with Wm. James, she is President of the Seventh Ward Primary Association.

"Mattie is a counselor to the President of all the Young Ladies Mutual Improvement Associations of the Church. When the *Woman's Exponent* was first published, Miss Mattie was the first girl to go into the printing office and learn type setting.

" Clara, the youngest, is accomplished, gifted spiritually, and an active worker. As her mother is often called from home by public duties, the charge of the home rests much of the time with her, a position she fills with dignity and ability."

Three babes died in infancy. And the mother of these children now honored among men and women, drove team hundreds of miles, not one journey, but many, and nearly always with a babe in her arms.

Resting now in the afternoon of life with comforts, honors and love surrounding her, Mrs. Horne must look back with satisfaction and gratitude upon her life. A few years ago, when I, a timid Secretary of the Fourteenth Ward Meetings, used to steal a look at her noble face, I used mentally to compare it to that of Washington, and I think still I was not mistaken; we, to-day, are struggling for "liberty to worship God according to the dictates of our own consciences," and the spirit of such as he and his co-laborers are with us and are ours, to counsel and to lead, through difficulties unto victory.

SARAH M. KIMBALL,

SECRETARY OF THE L. D. S. WOMEN'S ORGANIZATIONS.

"I am the daughter of Oliver Granger and Lydia Dibble Granger, was born December 29th, 1818, in the town of Phelps, Ontario Co., New York. Of my parents, eight children, only myself and two younger brothers, Lafayette and Farley, remain. My father, Oliver Granger, had an interesting experience in connection with the coming forth of the Book of Mormon. He obtained the book a few months after its publication, and while in the city of New York, at Prof. Mott's Eye Infirmary he had a 'heavenly vision.' My father was told of a personage who said his name was Moroni, that the Book of Mormon, about which his mind was exercised, was a true record of great worth, and Moroni instructed him (my father) to testify of its truth and that he should hereafter be ordained to preach the everlasting Gospel to the children of men. Moroni instructed my father to kneel and pray; Moroni and another personage knelt with him by the bedside. Moroni repeated words and instructed my father to repeat them after him. Moroni then stepped behind my father, who was still kneeling, and drew his finger over the three back seams of my father's coat, (which my father felt very perceptibly) and said, 'A time will come when the Saints will wear garments made without seams.' Moroni told my father that he might ask for what he most desired and it would be granted. He asked for an evidence by which he might know when he was approved of God. The evidence or sign was given, and remained with him until his dying hour, being more particularly manifest when engaged in prayer and meditation I love the memory of my father. He died in Kirtland, Ohio, August 1843, aged forty-seven.

I was married in Kirtland, Orange Co., Ohio, by Warren
Cowdery, Esq., September 23rd, 1840, to Hiram Kimball,
eldest son of Phineas and Abigail Kimball, of West Fairley,
Orange Co., Vermont. My parents had previously spent a
year in Nauvoo, Hancock Co., Ill.; their present stay in Ohio
was considered only temporary; my father sickened and died
there the next year. I returned with my husband to his
home in Nauvoo, Ill., three weeks after my marriage. We
boarded six months in the family of Dr. Frederick Williams,
then went to housekeeping. My eldest son was born in Nauvoo, November 22nd, 1841; when the babe was three days
old a little incident occurred which I will mention. The walls
of the Nauvoo Temple were about three feet above the foundation. The Church was in need of help to assist in raising the
Temple walls. I belonged to the Church of Jesus Christ of
Latter-Day Saints; my husband did not belong to the Church
at that time. I wished to help on the Temple, but did not
like to ask my husband (who owned considerable property) to
help for my sake. My husband came to my bedside, and as
he was admiring our three days' old darling, I said, "What is
the boy worth?" He replied, "O, I don't know, he is worth
a great deal." I said, "Is he worth a thousand dollars?"
The reply was, "Yes, more than that if he lives and does
well." I said, "Half of him is mine, is it not?" "Yes, I
suppose so." "Then I have something to help on the Temple." He said pleasantly, "You have?" "Yes, and I think of
turning my share right in as tithing." "Well, I'll see about
that." Soon after the above conversation Mr. Kimball met
the Prophet Joseph Smith, President of the Church, and said,
"Sarah has got a little the advantage of me this time, she
proposes to turn out the boy as Church property." President
Smith seemed pleased with the joke, and said, "I accept all
such donations, and from this day the boy shall stand recorded, *Church property.*" Then turning to Willard Richards,
his secretary, he said, "Make a record of this, and you are my
witness." Joseph Smith then said, "Major, (Mr. Kimball
was major in the Nauvoo Legion) you now have the privilege
4

of paying $500 and retaining possession, or receiving $500 and giving possession. " Mr. Kimball asked if city property was good currency, President Smith replied that it was. Then said Mr. Kimball, " How will that reserve block north of the Temple suit ? " President Smith replied, "It is just what we want. " The deed was soon made out and tranferred in due for ". President Smith said to me, " You have consecrated your first born son, for this you are blessed of the Lord. I bless you in the name of the Lord God of Abraham, of Isaac and of Jacob. And I seal upon you all the blessings that pertain to the faithful. Your name shall be handed down in honorable remembrance from generation to generation.

" Your son shall live and be a blessing to you in time, and an honor and glory to you throughout the endless eternities (changes) to come. He shall be girded about with righteousness and bear the helmet and the breast-plate of war. You shall be a blessing to your companion, and the honored mother of a noble posterity. You shall stand as a savior to your father's house, and receive an everlasting salvation, which I seal upon you by the gift of revelation and by virtue and authority of the holy priesthood vested in me, in the name of Jesus Christ. "

"Early in the year 1842, Joseph Smith taught me the principle of marriage for eternity, and the doctrine of plural marriage. He said that in teaching this he realized that he jeopardized his life; but God had revealed it to him many years before as a privilege with blessings, now God had revealed it again and instructed him to teach it with commandment, as the Church could travel (progress) no further without the introduction of this principle. I asked him to teach it to some one else. He looked at me reprovingly, and said, ' Will you tell me who to teach it to? God required me to teach it to you, and leave you with the responsibility of believing or disbelieving. ' He said, ' I will not cease to pray for you, and if you will seek unto God in prayer you will not be led into temptation.' "

" In the summer of 1843, a maiden lady (Miss Cook) was seamstress for me, and the subject of combining our efforts for

assisting the Temple hands came up in conversation. She
desired to be helpful but had no means to furnish. I told her
I would furnish material if she would make some shirts for
the workmen. It was then suggested that some of our neigh-
bors might wish to combine means and efforts with ours, and
we decided to invite a few to come and consult with us on the
subject of forming a Ladies' Society. The neighboring sisters
met in my parlor and decided to organize. I was delegated to
call on Sister Eliza R. Snow and ask her to write for us a
constitution and by-laws, and submit them to President Joseph
Smith prior to our next Thursday's meeting. She cheerfully
responded, and when she read them to him he replied that
the constitution and by-laws were the the best he had ever
seen. 'But,' he said, 'this is not what you want. Tell the
sisters their offering is accepted of the Lord, and He has
something better for them than a written constitution. I invite them all to meet me and a few of the brethren in the
Masonic Hall over my store next Thursday afternoon, and I
will organize the sisters under the priesthood after the pattern
of the priesthood.' He further said, 'The Church was
never perfectly organized until the women were thus organized.'" He wished to have Sister Emma Smith elected to
preside in fulfillment of the revelation which called her an
Elect Lady.

"In the wanderings and persecutions of the Church I have
participated, and in the blessings, endowments and holy an-
nointings and precious promises I have also received. To
sorrow I have not been a stranger; but I only write this short
sketch to instruct and happify, so I will skip to Salt Lake
City, September, 1851, with my two sons, Hiram and Oliver,
my widowed mother, Lydia Dibble Granger, Anna Robbins,
a girl that lived with me nine years and married my youngest
brother, and my two brothers, Lafayette and Farley B.
Granger. My husband was detained in New York City, and
had become financially much embarrassed. The next year
he came to me financially ruined and broken in health. I
engaged in school teaching in the Fourteenth Ward to sustain

and educate my family. My salary was only $25.00 per month, but that was much to us at that time.

"April 1st, 1854, my youngest son was born. I discontinued school three months, then opened school in my home. I taught eight years. I should have stated that on arriving here I sold our fitout (team, etc.) for a comfortable little home, this I have always considered providential. The Indian agent gave me a nine-year-old wild Indian girl, whom I educated and raised. She died at nineteen. I named her Kate.

"My mother who had lived with me twenty years, died in 1861, aged seventy-three. My husband was drowned March 1st, 1863, in the Pacific Ocean by the wreck of the steamer, *Ada Hancock*, off the coast of San Pedro, on his way to the Sandwich Islands; aged sixty-two.

"I was elected President of the Fifteenth Ward Relief Society February 7th, 1857. In December, 1865, a little girl was brought to me whom I adopted.

"November 13th, 1868, a silver trowel and mallet were furnished me and assisted by a Master Mason, and surrounded by an assemblage of people, I had the honor of laying the corner stone of the first Relief Society building erected in this dispensation."

Sister Sarah M. Kimball possesses a tall, commanding figure, a face of remarkable dignity and sincerity in expression. Her manner of speaking is original in its strength of reason, rare in its eloquence, precise and delicate in selection of words and tone of voice. A phrenologist once said of her, that "if she were seated in a railway carriage with parties on one hand discussing fashions, and politics to be heard on the other, she would turn to the discussion on politics." A statesman, a philanthropist, a missionary, in her very nature, she is none the less the noble mother and true, fond friend, to those who have known her longest and best.

PRESCENDIA L. KIMBALL.

In attempting a brief sketch of this noble woman's life, it is not necessary for me to state in regard to her ancestry, more than to say she is the elder sister of Mrs. Zina D. Young, the same genealogical references will suffice for both.

" Prescendia Lathrop Huntington was the fourth child of her parents, and was born in Watertown, Jefferson County, New York, September 10th, 1810. Mrs. Kimball is said to be the exact counterpart of the Eliza Huntington whose likeness is in the book, the record of the Huntingtons, as a type of the race. Sister Prescindia is a woman to see once, is to remember always. She reminds one of the dames of olden times, large, tall, grand and majestic in figure, dignified in manner, yet withal so womanly and sympathetic that she seems the embodiment of the motherly element to a degree that would embrace all who came under her influence. "

" Prescendia Huntington was married at the age of seventeen to Mr. Norman Buell. Their first child, George, was born in Mannsville, December 12th, 1823. Soon after they moved to Pinbury, Lewis County, where they made a comfortable home. Here their second son was born, December 25th, 1831, and in November 1833, by an accident was so severely burned that he died. In 1835, her mother came to visit her, and brought her the first intelligence of the Prophet Joseph and the record from the hill Cumorah. They sold their property the following winter and by spring reached Kirtland, Ohio. June 1st, 1836, Sister Prescendia was baptized and confirmed by Oliver Cowdery, and on the 9th her husband received the same ordinance. April 24th, 1838, her first daughter was born in a tumble-down dwelling on the Fishing River, Clay County, Mo., but lived only four hours. Here on two occasions she without protection, encountered an armed mob, but was saved from their hatred; they left her. Her husband had by this time apostatized. The Huntingtons were obliged to leave Far West at the time of the driving of the Saints from Missouri in the spring of 1839, and Sister Prescendia felt entirely alone and forsaken. She says, 'there was not at this time, one Saint in Missouri, to my knowledge.' About this time was born her son Oliver, just after the dreadful outrages perpetrated against the Saints in Missouri. In the fall of 1840 Mrs. Buell moved from Missouri and settled between Quincy and Nauvoo. During the ensuing five or six years she made frequent visits to the Saints, among others the families of Joseph and Hyrum, and Father and Mother Smith. Joseph himself taught her the principle of plural marriage. The sisters who had entered into these covenants were in one sense separate and apart from all others. No tongue can describe, or pen portray the peculiar situation of these noble, self-sacraficing women, who through the providence of God helped to establish the principle of celestial marriage The crisis came when the Prophet and Patriarch were foully murdered.

"The time came for the performances of the ordinances in the Temple at Nauvoo. Sister Prescendia availed herself of the privilege to go and receive her blessinge. Hereafter we recognize her as the wife of the Apostle, Heber C. Kimball. The next great event in the history of this people was the exodus from Nauvoo. The Saints had nearly all left for the West; Sister Prescendia felt as if she were at the mercy of the mob, and indeed, plans were laid to destroy her. As if in answer to her prayers, her brother, William, sent her a messenger telling her to leave all and come. On the 2nd of May, 1846, she walked out of her house leaving all behind her, taking her little boy who was sick and not able to be up but she was flying for her life. With the help of her son, George, she got away. She traveled all night, and reached a friend, Dr. Spurgeon, by daybreak. Took some refreshment and went into the woods with her little boy, staying all day, fasting and praying for deliverance. She says: 'I picked flowers for him and gave him water from the running stream. At night I went back to the doctor's, sleeping with my sick boy on a little bed on the floor. Next day I hid in a wagon. When we arrived at Nashville, I saw a man whom I knew, looking for me. 'I learned afterward he intended taking my child from me. My brother, Dimick, sent his sons to see me safely out of Illinois. I stayed in a deep ravine while some things were brought to me, and slept on a buffalo robe on the ground at night with my little child. No tongue can tell my feelings in those days of trial; but I had considered well, and felt I would rather suffer and die with the Saints, than live in Babylon as I had lived before. We arrived at Bonaparte. The excitement and exposure brought on fever and I was very ill. We at last arrived at Mt. Pisgah; there I found my father, my sister, Zina, and her children. They were in a log house without chimney or floor; sickness prevailed. Very soon men were sent by the Government to get volunteers to march to Mexico; to fight for a Government that had suffered us to be driven out at the point of the bayonet. * * I saw the five hundred men enrolled as volunteers to take up the line of march to Mexico. My brother, Dimick, brave-hearted and strong, with his family, among the number. His wife, Fanny, had a daughter born under most trying and painful circumstances. I was left behind at what was then called Cutler's Park. My father and Zina were at Mt. Pisgah. My brother, Dimick, in Mexico, my brother, William, in St. Louis, my brother, Oliver, on a mission in Europe; then came the news that my father had died at Pisgah; my friend, my counselor, my own dear parent, to whom I had looked for counsel for the future that stretched out before me like a great, unknown desert, unrelieved and barren. I had only my Heavenly Father left, and I reached out in faith to the One above to open the heavens for me and aid me in my loneliness. I was in a new, wild country without means. Joseph and Henry Woodmansee wanted me to keep house for them. As soon as I was settled their father wrote for them, and I was left in charge of their house. I started a school which was a great blessing to the children. The house was built of logs and covered with dirt and straw, with a little straw upon the floor. '

"Here Sister Prescendia toiled with scanty fare, teaching the children, and when school was closed for the night her voice would leave her, from weakness, but she loved the children and gained their affection. It was an ague country, provisions were scarce, lack of vegetables and fruit caused sickness. After a painful and dangerous illness, Sister Prescendia recovered her health About this time three brethren who went with the Mormon Batallion, came back to Winter Quarters, having been sent on special business from Pueblo. Says Sister Prescendia, 'I never saw such a pitiful sight before as these poor, worn-out travelers presented. Their clothing hung in rags, their faces burned, and with sun and snow they were nearly blind. Their feet were wrapped in rawhide from the buffalo. I sat and heard them tell how fearfully they had suffered crossing the prairies in the dead of winter, and all this in defence of a Government that had driven us defenceless women and children into a strange wilderness. I could not refrain from weeping when I looked upon these my brethren and realized how they. had suffered. '

"Early in the spring a few pioneers left to search out a haven of refuge for the Saints. The sisters left almost alone, lived near to God. They used often to meet together and pray. The gifts of tongues, interpretation and prophecy were given them at this time for their consolation. In May, 1846, Sister Prescendia and her little son, Oliver, left Winter Quarters. She, like many others, had to drive team, yoke cattle, &c., though in delicate health. She arrived in Salt Lake Valley September 22nd, and moved into the old Fort. January 6th, 1848, Sister Prescendia had born to her a daughter. The baby was a great comfort to the lonely mother who had left her home and come thousands of miles away. No daughter was ever more fondly loved than this little one.

"She was named Prescendia Celestia, and was rightly named Celestia, for she was more like a celestial being than a mortal one. President Young once asked her name; quick as thought, he said, ' *Celestial Prescendia.* '. Coming here as the Saints did provided with only the barest necessities, there was much privation to contend against. The families of Brigham and Heber shared in these respects equally with the others. When Sister Prescendia's babe was quite small, she had to put up an umbrella over them in bed to protect them from the rain. Sister Prescendia was patient and thanked her Father in heaven that he had permitted her to gather to the Rocky Mountains, and also that she had been permitted to become a mother under the new and everlasting covenant of marriage." Nothing could be more affecting than her story of the loss of this lovely child. She dressed her for a visit, and gave her in charge of her brother, while she finished her preparations. He took her to the family of President Young, and as they were seated at table, each gave her a kiss, admiring her beauty, President Young last.

"Returning to the mother, he sat her down a moment to cut a willow from the water's edge, and turning to her—she was gone. The sweet face, that going out smiled such a tender good-bye, was brought in cold in death. Vilate, the first wife of Heber, said, "The flower of the flock is gone." Years have passed since then, but the beauty of that little face is undimmed in her mother's memory."

Sister Prescendia was for fifteen years secretary of the Sixteenth Ward Relief Society.

Sister Prescendia's labors have been in the House of the Lord, and annointing and administering to the sick. Hundreds have asked for her presence at their bedside—the name, Prescendia—has been almost like that sweet word, *mother.* I reflect upon the lonely, trial path that she has trod, the wounds her heart has borne; and listening to the tender pathos of her voice, the sublimity of her words; the nobility of her life commanding my love and reverence.

If I could choose the picture which should be historical, it should be as I have seen her; standing, her grand figure becomingly wrapped in a large, circular cloak, a handsome, large black bonnet shielding her venerable and beloved face

5

from the falling flakes of snow. Looking upon her I thought her the very picture of a Puritan exile, a revolutionary ancestress, and a Latter-Day Saint veteran and pioneer. I shall always remember her thus, it is an ineffacable picture in my memory.

Since writing the above, the following appears in the *Deseret News* of September 11th:

"MANIFESTATION OF RESPECT.

" Yesterday being the anniversary of the birthday of Sister Prescendia L. Kimball, a party of ladies numbering about thirty, of her personal friends, mostly of very long standing, assembled at her residence. A lunch was partaken of about noon, and subsequently the gathering took the form of a meeting, at which all present expressed themselves appropriately to the occasion. The sisters also presented the venerable and respected lady, a handsome black satin cloak, trimmed with fur and lined with crimson plush, for winter wear. We are pleased to be able to state that Sister Kimball's health has considerably improved during the last few days. "

PHŒBE W. CARTER WOODRUFF,

WIFE OF WILFORD WOODRUFF, PRESIDENT OF THE TWELVE
APOSTLES, OF THE CHURCH OF JESUS CHRIST OF LATTER-
DAY SAINTS.

"I, Phœbe W. Carter, wife of Apostle Wilford Woodruff,
was born in Scarboro, in the State of Maine, March 8th, 1807.
My father was of English descent, coming to America at
about the close of the seventeenth century. My mother,
Sarah Fabyan, was also of England, and of the third generation from England. The name of Fabyan is ancient, and of a
noble family. My father's family, also, much of the old
Puritan stamp.

"In the year 1834, I embraced the Gospel, as revealed
through the Prophet Joseph Smith, and, about a year after,
I left my parents and kindred, and journeyed to Kirtland,
Ohio, a distance of one thousand miles, a lone maid, sustained
only by my faith and trust in Israel's God. My friends mar-
velled at my course, as did I, but something within impelled
me on. My mother's grief at my leaving home was almost
more than I could bear; and had it not been for the spirit
within I should have faltered at the last. My mother told me
she would rather see me buried than going thus alone into the
heartless world, and especially was she concerned about my
leaving home to cast my lot among the Mormons. 'Phœbe,'
she said, impressively, 'will you come back to me if you find
Mormonism false?' I answered thrice, 'Yes, mother, I will.'
These were my words well remembered to this day; she
knew I would keep my promise. My answer relieved her
trouble; but it cost us all much sorrow to part. When the
time came for my departure I dared not trust myself to say

farewell, so I wrote my good-bye to each, and leaving them on my table, ran down stairs and jumped into the carriage. Thus I left my beloved home of childhood to link my life with the Saints of God.'

"When I arrived in Kirtland I became acquainted with the Prophet Joseph Smith, and received more evidence of his divine mission. There in Kirtland I formed the acquaintance of Elder Wilford Woodruff, to whom I was married in 1836. With him I went to the 'Islands of the Sea' and to England, on misisons. Here I will bear my testimony to the power of God which I have often seen manifested among the Latter-Day Saints. The following is one notable instance:

"When the Saints were settling Nauvoo, the unhealthy labor of breaking new land on the banks of the Mississippi for the founding of the city, invited pestilence. Nearly everyone was attacked with fever and ague. The Prophet had the sick borne into his house and dooryard until the place was like a hospital. At length even he succumbed to the deadly contagion and for several days was as helpless as the rest of our people, who were all nearly exhausted by their extermination from Missouri. But the spirit of the Lord came down upon Joseph, commanding him to arise and stay the pestilence. The Prophet arose from his bed and the power of God rested upon him. He commenced in his own house and dooryard, commanding the sick in the name of Jesus Christ to arise and be made whole; and they were healed according to his word. He then continued to travel from house to house, and from tent to tent, upon the bank of the river, healing the sick as he went, until he arrived at the upper stone house, where he crossed the river in a boat accompanied by several of the Quorum of the Twelve, whom he had bade to follow him, and landed in Montrose. He walked into the cabin of Brigham Young, who was lying sick, and commanded him in the name of Jesus Christ to arise and be made whole, and follow him, which he did. They came to our house next, and Joseph bade Mr. Woodruff, also, to follow, and then they went to the house of Brother Elijah Fordham, who was supposed by his family and friends to have been dying, for two weeks. The Prophet stepped to his bedside, took him by the hand, and commanded him in the name of Jesus Christ to arise from his bed and be made whole. His voice, Joseph Smith's, was as the voice of God. Brother Fordham instantly leaped from his bed, called for his clothing and dressed himself, and followed the Apostles into the street. They then went into the house of Joseph B. Nobles, who lay very sick, and he was healed in like manner. And when by the power of God granted unto him, Joseph had healed all the sick, he recrossed the river and returned to his own house. Thousands of witnesses bear testimony of the miracle. It was a day never to be forgotten. Hearing of the case of Brother Fordham, whom I with the rest had believed to be dying, I thought I would go and see with my own eyes. I found him very happy, sitting in his chair. He told me he had been out to work in his garden. This was only a few hours after the miracle. From that day I never doubted that this was the work of God.

"It will be expected that I should say something on polygamy. I have this to say. When the principle of plural marriage was first taught, I thought it was the most wicked thing I ever heard of; consequently I opposed it to the best of my ability, until I became sick and wretched. As soon, however, as I became convinced that it originated as a revelation from God through Joseph, knowing him to be a prophet, I wrestled with my Heavenly Father in fervent prayer, to be guided aright at that all-important moment of my life. The answer came. Peace was given to my mind. I knew it was the will of God; and from that time to the present I have sought to faithfully honor the patriarchal law.

"Of Joseph, my testimony is that he was one of the greatest prophets the Lord ever called, that he lived for the redemption of mankind and died a martyr for the truth. The love of the Saints for him will never die.

"It was after the martyrdom of Joseph that I accompanied my husband to England in 1845. On our return the advance companies of the Saints had left Nauvoo under President

Young and others of the Twelve. We followed immediately and journeyed to Winter Quarters. The next year my husband went with the pioneers to the mountains while the care of the family rested on me. After his return and the re-organization of the First Presidency, I accompanied my husband on his mission to the Eastern States. In 1850 we arrived in the Valley and since that time Salt Lake City has been my home.

" Of my husband, I can truly say I have found him a worthy man with scarcely his superior on earth. He has built up a branch of the Church wherever he has labored. He has been faithful to God and his family, every day of his life. My respect for him has increased with our years, and my desire for an eternal union with him will be the last wish of my mortal life. "

At the first organization of the Relief Society in the Fourteeth Ward, in the spring of 1857, Mrs. Woodruff was chosen by Bishop A. Hoagland as President, which position she held until by the "move" south, the society was discontinued. After their return she was invited to resume her position, but so much of the family care and management of business devolved upon her as her husband's faithful partner, that she felt she could not do justice to that object, and Bishop Hoagland asked her to nominate her successor. She chose her first counselor, Mary Isabella Horne. Mrs. Woodruff is also one of the presiding board of six, over the General Retrenchment Meetings, held semi-monthly in the Fourteenth Ward. In May, 1882, Mrs. Woodruff was elected one of the Executive Board of the Deseret Hospital. She often accompanies Apostle Wilford Woodruff on his visits among the settlements, holding meetings with the sisters, who look upon her as one of the wisest women in the knowledge of the Scriptures and in her counsels among her sisters in the *Church*. The record of her life and labors would make a deeply interesting volume which could not fail to inspire the youth of Zion with a desire to emulate her worthy example, and the hearts of older ones with admiration and reverence. The eighteen years of our acquaintance have served to strengthen and beautify my friendship for Phœbe W. Woodruff, as wife, mother and Saint. It seems but fitting, to record here that the mother and father of Sister Woodruff were baptized by Apostle Wilford Woodruff. Thus ended all the fears of the Puritan mother.

Quoting an historian of note (himself an occupant of part of the Woodruff residence for a long period): "Sister Phœbe W. Woodruff is one of the noblest examples of her sex,— truly a mother in Israel; and in her strength of character, consistency and devotion, she has but few peers in the Church."

BATHSHEBA W. SMITH.

WIFE OF APOSTLE GEORGE A. SMITH, OF REVERED MEMORY,
WHO WAS ONE OF THE FIRST PRESIDENCY OF THE CHURCH
OF LATTER-DAY SAINTS.

Bathsheba W. Smith is the daughter of Mark and Susannah
Bigler, and was born at Shirnsten, Harrison Co., West Virginia, on May 3rd, 1822. Her father was from Pennsylvania,
her mother from Maryland. The school facilities in her vicinity were limited. The county of Harrison was hilly, and
the roads of primitive character; the mode of travel was
chiefly on horseback riding, in which few could excel her.

In her girlhood she was religiously inclined, loved virtue,
honesty, truthfulness and integrity; attended secret prayers,
studied to be cheerful, industrious and happy, and was always
opposed to rudeness.

During her fifteenth year some Latter-Day Saints visited
the neighborhood, she heard them preach and believed what
they taught. She knew by the spirit of the Lord, in answer
to her prayer, that Joseph Smith was a prophet of the Lord,
and that the Book of Mormon was a divine record. On the
21st of August, 1837, Bathsheba W. Bigler was baptized into
the Church of Jesus Christ, and the most of her father's family
also, about the same time. They soon felt a desire to gather
with the rest of the Saints in Missouri, her sister, Nancy, and
family sold their property, intending to go in the fall, and
Bathsheba was very anxious to go with them. Her father
having not yet sold out his property, she was told she could
not go. This caused her to retire very early, feeling very
sorrowful. While weeping, a voice said to her, " Weep not,
you will go this fall." She was comforted and perfectly sat-

isfied, and the next morning testified to what the voice had said to her.

Soon after, her father sold his home and they all went to Missouri, to her great joy, but on their arrival there found the State preparing to war against the Saints. A few nights before they reached Far West, they camped with a company of eastern Saints, but separated on account of each company choosing different ferries. The company Sister Bathsheba and her family were in, arrived safely at their destination, but the others were overtaken by an armed mob; seventeen were killed, others were wounded, and some maimed for life. In a few days after their arrival there was a battle between the Saints and the mob, in which David W. Patten (one of the first Twelve Apostles,) was wounded, and he was brought to the house where they were stopping. Sister Bathsheba witnessed his death a few days after, and saw thousands of mobbers arrayed against the Saints, and heard their dreadful threats and savage yells, when our Prophet Joseph and his brethren were taken into their camp. The Prophet, Patriarch and many others were taken to prison; and the Saints had to leave the State. In the spring they had the joy of having the prophet and his brethren restored to them at Quincy, Illinois.

In the spring of 1840, the family of Sister Bathsheba moved to Nauvoo, where she had many opportunities of hearing the Prophet Joseph preach, and tried to profit by his instructions, and also received many testimonies of the truths which he taught.

On the 25th of July, 1841, Bathsheba W. Bigler was married to George A. Smith, the then youngest member of the Twelve Apostles, Elder Don Carlos Smith (brother of the prophet) officiating. George A. Smith was own cousin to the Prophet Joseph. When Sister Bathsheba first became acquainted with George A. Smith he was the junior member of the First Quorum of Seventies. On the 26th of June, 1838, he was ordained a member of the High Council of Adam Ondi Ahman, in Davis County, Missouri. Just about the break of day on the 26th of April, 1834, while kneeling on the corner stone of the

6

foundation of the Lord's House at Far West, Caldwell County, Missouri, he was ordained one of the Twelve Apostles, and from thence started on a mission to Europe, from which he returned ten days previous to their marriage.

As the 4th of July, 1842, came on the Sabbath day, they celebrated the anniversary on Monday the 5th. There was a military display of the Nauvoo Legion, and a sham battle fought. George A. Smith was in the general's staff in the uniform of a chaplain. Sister Bathsheba watched the proceedings with great interest. On the 7th of July a son was born to them; they named him George Albert. Two months after, George A., as the Saints loved to call him, went on a mission to the Eastern States. On his previous mission (to England,) he injured his left lung, causing hemmorhage. In the fall of 1843, George A. and Bathsheba received their endowments and were united under the holy order of celestial marriage. Sister Bathsheba heard the Prophet Joseph charge the Twelve with the duty and responsibility of the ordinances of endowments and sealing, for the living and the dead. Sister Bathsheba met many times with her husband, Joseph and others who had received their endowments, in an upper room dedicated for the purpose, and prayed with them repeatedly in those meetings. In the spring of 1844, Mr. Smith went on another mission, and soon after he left persecution began in the city of Nauvoo which ended in the martyrdom of our beloved prophet and patriarch. Mr. Smith returned about the 1st of August, and on the 14th a daughter was born, and they named her Bathsheba.

Having become thoroughly convinced that the doctrine of plurality of wives was from God, and firmly believing that she should participate with him in all his blessings, glory and honor, Sister Bathsheba gave to her husband different wives during the year of his return home. She says of this; "Being proud of my husband and loving him very much, knowing him to be a man of God, and having a testimony that what I had done was acceptable to my Father in heaven, I was as happy as I knew how to be."

It would be in vain to describe how they traveled through snow, wind and rain, how roads had to be made, bridges built and rafts constructed, how our poor animals had to drag on day after day with scanty food; nor how we suffered from poverty, sickness and deaths, but the Lord was with us, His power was made manifest daily. Quoting from her, "My dear mother died on the 11th of March, 1844, and on the 4th of April I had a son born who lived but four hours." They arrived in Salt Lake Valley (now city) in October, 1849, after traveling over sterile deserts and plains, over high mountains and through deep canyons, ferrying some streams and fording others, but all was joy now. Sister Bathsheba went to her sister's house, and O, how delightful it did seem to be once more in a comfortable room with a blazing fire on the hearth, where the mountain's rude blasts nor the desert's wild winds could not reach them.

In March, 1850, Sister Bathsheba moved into their own house. In December, 1850, George A. Smith was called to go south to found a settlement in Little Salt Lake Valley, two hundred and fifty miles from home. In 1851, he returned, having been elected a member of the Legislature from Iron Co. In 1856, he was sent to Washington to ask for the admission of Utah as a State. In May, 1857, he returned to Utah. In 1858, they went south, bidding farewell to their home, feeling as they did on leaving Nauvoo; that they should never see it again, fleeing as they were, before the approaching army.

However, President Buchanan sent out his Peace Commissioners who brought his Proclamation, declaring a general amnesty to all offenders. Peace being restored, they returned to Salt Lake City in July, having been gone three months. When they entered the city it was almost sundown; all was quiet, every door was boarded up. From only two or three chimneys smoke was rising. How still and lonely, yet the breath of peace wafted over the silent city, and it was home! They had left a partly finished house, and resuming work upon it, by October it was finished. Sister Bathsheba says: "It was so comfortable and we were so happy! We had plenty of room. My son and daughter took great pleasure in having their associates come and visit them frequently. They would have a room full of company, and would engage in reading useful books, singing, playing music, dancing, &c. My son played the flute, flutina and was a good drummer. My son and daughter were good singers, they made our home joyous with song and jest." In 1860, this son was sent on a mission to the Moquois Indians. He was interested in this and apt in learning the language. After being set apart by the authorities for that mission, he started on the 4th of September, and had traveled about seven hundred miles, when on the 2nd of November he was killed by Navajo Indians. On the 3rd of January the daughter was married.

In 1873, Sister Bathsheba made a tour with her husband and President Young and party, to the Colorado and up the Rio Virgen as far as Shonesberg. In 1872, they made another tour with President Young and party, visiting at St. George, Virgen City, Long Valley and Kanab. In 1873, went again with her husband, President Young and company and spent the winter in St. George, going by way of San Pete and Sevier counties. During this journey Sister Bathsheba attended several meetings with the sisters, returning home April, 1874. She has visited the Saints as far south as the junction of the Rio Virgen with the Colorado, has visited the settlements on the Muddy River, and also the Saints as far north as Bear Lake and Soda Springs. On their travels they have often been met by bands of music, and thousands of children bearing banners and flags; and singing songs of welcome. Sister Bathsheba has enjoyed these tours very much. She has accompanied many explorations down into deep gulches to see the water pockets, over beautiful plains in carriages or cars, and over mountains and deserts.

In reference to her position in duties of a public and spiritual character, we find the following: Returning from a tour, February 19th, 1878, they arrived in Salt Lake City, finding all safe at home. I quote again from Sister Bathsheba's journal, written in her own hand:

"My dear husband was not well; I thought I could soon nurse him up to health, but my efforts were all in vain, he expired on the first of September after a long sickness." The departure was a shock to many. For many months prayers had been offered up through all parts of the Territory, for the restoration to health of this great and good man. Seated in his chair, his faithful wife beside him, he turned from his conversation with President Young and others who constantly attended him, and leaning upon her devoted heart breathed his last.

Sister Bathsheba W. Smith belonged to the first Relief Society which was organized at Nauvoo, and was present when it was organized, the Prophet Joseph presiding. Officiated as Priestess in the Nauvoo Temple. Was Secretary in the Seventeenth Ward Relief Society, Salt Lake City; had been First Counselor to President Rachel Grant in the Relief Society of the Thirteenth Ward, Salt Lake City, for many years. Is a Counselor to M. I. Horne in the General Retrenchment Association, Fourteenth Ward, and is also Treasurer of the Relief Society of the Salt Lake Stake. Has officiated in the holy ordinances of the House of the Lord in Salt Lake City for many years. Is also one of the Board of Directors in the Deseret Hospital. She says, "I have attended many meetings of the sisters and had many seasons of rejoicing."

Sister Bathsheba is often reverently spoken of as "the beloved wife of George A. Smith." To her, in one sense, this would be the dearest praise that could be spoken. But yet a loftier, holier, than even the earth-love seems to hover around her very presence. A little child once said, "When I look at Sister Bathsheba, I do not see her with her bonnet on, I see her as she will look when she wears that crown that is waiting for her." Such is the impression her face, her gentle voice and manner convey. To the record of her life, and this, I could add nothing.

ELIZABETH HOWARD.

SECRETARY OF THE RELIEF SOCIETIES OF THE SALT LAKE STAKE
OF ZION.

Mrs. Howard furnishes a very brief sketch for one whose
life and labors among the people and faith of her adoption,
have been so extended, important and interesting, to all who
have ever come within the influence of her noble, generous
spirit; who have received the stimulus to failing spirits and
energy which emanated from her animated face, so good and
motherly, her voice so cheerful and sympathetic, and her
every movement like an inspiration of strength, happiness
and life;

She writes she was " descended from Scotch parentage on
her father's side, Irish on her mother's, Websters and Wards.
Was born on July 12th, 1823, at Carlow, Carlow County, Ire-
land." Was the first child of her parents and says she "had
a glorious childhood and girlhood," which can be easily believed, judging by her ever bouyant spirits. She was "married
to William Howard, the eldest son of Stott and Catherine
Howard, June 9th, 1841. Heard the Gospel in 1851, and
came to America in 1853, with husband, two sons, four daughters, two hired girls and two hired men." They arrived in
Utah, September, 1853.

At the organizations of the Relief Society in 1867-68, she
was appointed Secretary of the Big Cottonwood Ward, which
office she filled until she accompanied her husband to England in 1868, returned in 1869 and resumed the same office.
During their mission in England, Mrs. Howard was often
called upon to explain the principles of our doctrines and

answer many questions regarding our people, etc. Divines and others found Mrs. Howard quite ready and able to meet and answer them on every point. It fact her part of the mission has often been referred to as something exceptionally creditable and important. It was at a time, too, when woman had scarcely been heard to speak upon our faith, outside the home circle.

About 1871, when Mrs. M. A. Smoot removed to Provo, Mrs. Howard was chosen Counselor to Mrs. M. I. Horne in the General Retrenchment Association, which position she still holds. When the Relief Societies were organized into Stakes. Mrs. Howard was appointed Secretary of the Salt Lake Stake of Zion, which position she holds at the present time. Mrs. Howard has traveled much throughout our Territory in company with other sisters, visiting the different societies and associations in a missionary capacity, giving instructions and infusing cheerfulness and energy by her whole-souled and genial manner. There is something wonderfully earnest and sincere in all she says and does, and it has a most convincing effect upon the hearers who delight to welcome her visits, who is herself a most delightful entertainer and hostess at her own beautiful country home a few miles ride out from the city.

Mrs. Howard is the mother of ten children, eight living; and thirty-seven grand-children.

ELMINA S. TAYLOR.

PRESIDENT OF THE YOUNG LADIES' MUTUAL IMPROVEMENT ASSOCIATIONS, OF THE CHURCH OF JESUS CHRIST OF LATTER-DAY SAINTS.

I was born at Middlefield, Otsego County, State of New York, September 12th, 1830. My parents are Daniel Shepard and Rozita Bailey Shepard. Three daughters were all the children that were born to them, I being the eldest. My parents were staunch Methodists, and I was brought up in that faith. I united myself with that church when about twenty years of age, and during some six years was a zealous and consistent member of the same. At the time I joined the Church I was desirous to be baptized by immersion as I considered that the pattern set by our Savior; although I had always been taught that baptism was not a saving ordinance, but only to answer a good conscience, otherwise, an outward sign of an inward grace. To this my many friends were so much opposed that after some time elapsed I consented, and was admitted a member of the church, by sprinkling; but there were many doctrines and tenets with which I never was satisfied, and when I went to my minister to have them explained 1 was more beclouded and found myself more in the dark than before; though I sought to the Lord earnestly to be guided aright.

"In the year 1854, circumstances induced me to go to Haverstraw, a large town situated in southern New York, on the banks of the beautiful Hudson River, to engage in teaching. One of the trustees, John Druce, was a Mormon elder, who had a very interesting and intelligent family. My cousin and I frequently visited there, but for a long time they never

mentioned religion to us, fearing to frighten us away, but one
night, just as I was leaving, he asked me if I would read some
Mormon books. I answered, "O, yes! You know the Bible
says prove all things and hold fast that which is good.' His
earnestness impressed me. Before opening the books I bowed
before the Lord and fervently implored Him to give me His
spirit that I might understand if they were true or false. My
interest was awakened, and the more I investigated and compared the doctrines with the Scriptures, the more I was convinced of their truth. I fought against my convictions, for I
well knew how it would grieve my dear parents to have me
unite myself with that despised people; and I also thought I
should lose my situation which was a very lucrative one.
However, I could not silence my convictious, and as the
promise was given, 'If you will obey the doctrine, you shall
know whether it is of God or man;' I went forth and was
baptized July 5th, 1856. When I was confirmed by the layling
on of hands I received the testimony of its truth which I have
never lost from that day to this.

"I was united in marriage to George Hamilton Taylor, August
31st, 1856, by Apostle, now President, John Taylor, and in
1859, April fifteenth, we left New York for Utah, where we
arrived September 16th of the same year, after a long tedious
journey with ox teams. In the spring of 1860 we located in
the Fourteenth Ward, where we have since resided, and
where our first child, a son, was born July 16th of the same
year. While in the States we were never blessed with
children, but it was prophesied upon my head that I should
go to Zion and should there be blessed with them, which has
been fulfilled, for I am now the mother of seven.

"Through the gift of tongues, it was also promised that all
my family should come to me, which was verified after we had
been here nearly fifteen years, and my father is still with us,
having reached the advanced age of seventy-nine years, but
none of them ever received the Gospel.

"At the organization of the Relief Society of the Fourteenth
Ward, December 12th, 1867, I was elected Secretary, an office
7

which I still occupy. September 23rd, 1874, by request of Sister E. R. S. Snow, I was appointed Superintendent of the Young Ladies' Association of the same ward. I was chosen First Counselor to Sister M. I. Horne, Stake President of Salt Lake County, December 22nd, 1879, and have traveled considerably in that capacity.

"At a Conference held in the Assembly Hall, Salt Lake City, June 19th, 1880, was appointed President of the Young Ladies Mutual Improvement Association of Zion.

"July 4th, 1877, we entered into the celestial order of marriage, and have since all lived under the same roof, and eaten at the same table, ever in the enjoyment of peace and harmony."

All who are acquainted with the writer of the above autobiographical sketch, can cheerfully add testimony to its concluding paragraph. "Love at Home" might be graven upon a tablet of stone within their door, so indelibly seems that sacred principle to have been impressed upon the hearts within that household.

By example, by attainments, and the spiritual refinement and elegance in bearing which would denote the christian lady, under any or all circumstances, it seems peculiarly appropriate that Mrs. Elmira S. Taylor was called to preside over the young ladies of Zion. May they emulate their standard, spiritually and socially. The simplicity and modesty of her sketch cannot convey to the mind of the reader those delicate attributes of character, so well understood by those who, like myself, have been recipients of her kindly counsels and encouragement, and recognized in a wider sense by those who have listened to her addresses, dictated by the spirit of our sacred and holy religion.

MARY A. FREEZE.

PRESIDENT OF THE Y. L. M. I. A. OF THE SALT LAKE STAKE OF ZION.

Mary A. Freeze is the daughter of James Lewis Burnham and his wife, Mary Ann, who were born in Vermont. In 1837, with their one child they emigrated to McHenry County, Illinois, where they made them a home, leaving there in 1843 for Beauro County in the same State. In the latter place they heard and obeyed the Gospel of Jesus Christ. Mr. Burnham was a minister of the Church called Christians, but after hearing the elders explain the principles of this Gospel, could not but acknowledge that he had no legal authority to preach, and consequently was baptized into the Church of Jesus Christ of Latter-Day Saints, whose doctrines he preached and advocated faithfully until the day of his death, from bleeding of the lungs, caused by preaching in the open air. In 1843, Mr. and Mrs. Burnham had moved to Nauvoo. They there had four children, the youngest, a little girl, died in 1844. Mr. Burnham labored as much as his failing strength would permit, quarrying rock for the Temple. In the summer of 1845 he grew worse. Mrs. Freeze says, "This was four days previous to my birth. This was a trying time for my mother, being left in sorrow and very destitute of worldly goods, with no relatives near to help her; but the Saints were very kind to her in her affliction. Her relatives in the East would gladly have sent means to take her back, but she had cast her lot with the Saints of God and preferred to remain with them in the depths of poverty than to have the wealth of the whole world, elsewhere. After the Temple was finished she entered therein, partaking of the ordinances, and was sealed to President Joseph Young, (brother of President Brigham Young,) he performing this ordinance for my father, who had died before the opportunity of this privilege.   She afterwards had two daughters who are now the wives of Robert N. Russell and Jasper Conrad.

"In February, 1846, the famous exodus began, but my mother had no way of going so remained until after the battle took place and the Saints were driven out on pain of losing their lives.   Mother received a wagon for her city property and was lent a yoke of oxen, that she might begin that memorable, toilsome journey with her four little children.   I have heard her tell of the mobs searching the wagons for arms, the obscene language they used, and how terribly she suffered from fear.   She arrived at Winter Quarters late in the fall, where she remained a year and a half, when they were compelled by the Government to move back on the east side of the river, because they were on Indian Territory.   Soon after this she let her second and third sons, Wallace and George, go on to the valley with Brother Daniel Woods.   This was a severe trial to my loving mother, but there seemed to be no other way for them to be taken care of as the Saints were in the deepest poverty.   I have often heard her and Brother Luther also, rehearse the want and distress they endured, sometimes nearly amounting to starvation.   We were compelled to remain there until 1852, when through the kindness of the brethren we were enabled in June to cross the plains, arriving in Salt Lake City, October 8th, last day of Conference. I was too young to remember much about the journey, but one circumstance impressed itself upon my mind.   While climbing into the wagon I fell, and was run over by both wheels and very badly hurt, but through the administration of the elders was almost instantly healed and felt no bad effects from the injury afterward.

"We located in Bountiful, Davis County, ten miles north of Salt Lake City, where we lived until I was sixteen years old. I was baptized when nine years of age and felt happy in the assurance that I was a 'Mormon' in very deed.   At the time of the Reformation, I was full of the inspiration of the times although only eleven years old, and was very much in earnest in repenting of my sins, and making new covenants to serve the Lord more faithfully in the future. During my early years I attended school the entire season, until old enough to assist my mother, when I attended during the winter only. Being very assiduous I acquired a good common school education. In 1861 we moved to Richmond, Cache Valley, my brothers having taken up land and made a home there. It was there I became acquainted with James Perry Freeze, whom I assisted in teaching school six months, not dreaming of the relationship I was destined to sustain to him. My girlhood days were not as happy as might have been, on account of our exceeding poverty, but I have many times since thought that it was for my greatest good that I was reared in want and loneliness; that it was a means of keeping me humble, the good spirit thereby finding a receptacle in my heart, giving me a desire to seek after truth and learn of the things of God. Had I possessed wealth and my mind been filled with the follies and fashions of the world, I might not have had such a desire to make the Lord my friend. At an early age I read in the Doctrine and Covenants, that God is no respecter of persons, but in all countries those who fear Him and work righteousness are accepted of Him. This was a great comfort to me, a guiding star to my whole future life; that by leading a righteous life I should be loved of my Father in heaven equally with the richest and most highly born; that possessing His love and favor I possessed everything worth caring for.

"In March, 1863, I was married to James P. Freeze, whom, I felt assured was a noble man, one that I could trust as the guardian of my life. I am the mother of eight children. We resided in Richmond six months after our marriage, when we came to Salt Lake City, where he has since followed the mercantile business. In 1864, we became identified with the Eleventh Ward where we still live. In 1871, I was called to preside over the Young Ladies Mutual Improvement Association of this Ward, accepting it with great reluctance, feeling my incapability, but have filled it to the best ability which

God has given me, and have proven that all who seek the Lord in humility, will surely receive a blessing at His hand. Through the blessing of the Almighty, I have now the love and confidence of the members who have manifested the same in various ways.

"In the spring of 1871, my husband, a faithful man, desirous of keeping all the commandments of God, saw fit, with my full consent, to take to himself another of the daughters of Eve, a good and worthy girl, Jane Granter by name. It tried my spirit to its utmost endurance, but I always believed the principle to be true, and felt that it was time we obeyed that sacred order. The Lord knew my heart and desires, and was with me in my trial and assisted me to overcome the selfishness and jealousy of my nature. With his help, added to the great kindness of my husband, who has ever stood at the head of his family as a wise and just man, I soon obtained peace. While undergoing the severest trial to my feelings, I was inspired with the following lines which the Lord was not slow to answer:

"'Father, help me to do Thy will,
Command my troubled heart be still;
Cause my soul with peace to flow,
While I sojourn here below,
Help me still to realize
Thou'rt the giver of the prize
That I would win through faithfulness.
Then, Father, O look down and bless
Thine erring child that cries to Thee
For help, amid life's stormy sea.'

"My husband has since taken two other wives, and I praise the Lord that I had so far overcome, that instead of feeling it to be a trial, it was a source of joy and pride that we were counted worthy to have such noble girls enter our family. The two last were my Counselors in the Young Ladies' Improvement Association of our Ward. I have loved the wives of my husband as I would have my own sisters, realizing that the power of the Holy Priesthood that has bound us together for time and eternity is stronger than kindred ties. Sophia lived with me nearly seven years; she died December, 1879, which was one of the greatest trials of my life. I could as willingly have parted with one of my own daughters. She left me a beautiful boy who seems as near to me as my own. I wish to bear testimony to my descendants, and to all who may read this sketch, that I know by the power of the Holy Ghost which bears testimony to my spirit, that the Patriarchal Order of Marriage is from God and was revealed for the exaltation and salvation of the human family, also that I have had peace, joy and satisfaction in living in that Order such as I had never known before; and have had many proofs that God will pour out His blessings upon those who keep His laws, seeking Him with full purpose of heart, for He will be sought after by His children.

"September 14, 1878, the authorities having considered it necessary to institute a Stake Organization of the Young Young Ladies' Mutual Improvement Association, I was chosen as President of these Associations in this Salt Lake Stake of Zion. I chose Louie Felt, and Clara Y. Conrad, my half-sister, as my Counselors. We have visited the Associations as far as practicable, have enjoyed the spirit of our mission and feel assured we have been instrumental in the hands of God of doing much good.

"I am striving to purify myself, and keep all of the commandments of God, to be diligent in the performance of every duty assisting to roll forth the great work our Father has established in the last days, that I may be worthy to receive the blessings which have been pronounced upon my head; for they are great and many, and I know I shall receive them if found worthy. I know the fruits of this Gospel are peace, joy and happiness, and all who obey its precepts will have in this life that peace which passeth all understanding, that which the world cannot give nor take away, and having finished their labors, and are called to another sphere, will be crowned with life eternal, which is the greatest of all gifts. It has been the greatest desire of my life that my children should become bright and shining lights in the church of God, and knowing that much depends upon parents, I have ever striven to set them an example worthy of imitation, teaching them true principles, that I might not come under condemnation for my neglect of duty.

"I realize that heaven would not be heaven to me if my children, through sin and transgression, could not have a place there; that my glory would be dimmed forever.

"I will now say good-bye, until we meet where there is neither sorrow nor mourning, but our joy will be perfect; and trust my descendants may all keep the laws of God, and be worthy to sit down with Abraham, Isaac and Jacob, Joseph Smith, Brigham Young and all the faithful in the kingdom of God, to go no more out."

Mrs. Freeze says, "We have traced our lineage back to the year 1200, and have the record of the same. We descended from the Normans. Our family was at one time very wealthy and numerous in England; there is a town which bears their name. Three brothers came to America at an early date, one settled in Vermont, and two in Massachusetts. Their descendants took part in the Revolutionary War, and among them according to the 'Burnham Record' were many Doctors of Divinity, Doctors of Law, and one Mary Burnham, writes of the 'service of gold, their equipages and household appointments, of that grandeur brought with them from their ancient and noble halls of England.' Several of the Burnham descendants were officers in the late Civil War in America."

Mrs. Freeze is of that class of spirits that (in religion or justice) opposition would animate, persecution, inspire her. I have often thought, looking into her eyes, that in their depths slumbered the embers (scarcely covered by the ashes of dead years) of the fires of patriot's and martyr's souls.

LOUIE FELT,

PRESIDENT OF THE PRIMARY ASSOCIATIONS OF THE CHURCH OF
JESUS CHRIST OF LATTER-DAY SAINTS.

Louie Felt was the daughter of Joseph and Mary Bouton,
was born in South Norfolk, Conn., May 5, 1852. Was baptized when eight years old and came to Utah in September,
1866. On December 29th of same year was married to Joseph H.
Felt. At the October Conference of 1867, they were called to
go on the Muddy River Mission and started the 9th of November following. They remained there between two and three
years, enduring many hardships; the heat in summer being
particularly trying to those used to a Northern clime. "Ninety
degrees in the shade" is considered high in our eastern cities,
but at the Muddy, for months it would rise above one hundred
degrees at midnight. The buildings were new, low adobe
houses, lumber scarce, and often the wife was asked, "where
would you prefer to have the boards, over your head or under
your feet?" Those who had babies to rock took the choice of
a floor, and put up with a thatched roof. The winds blew with
great violence, and the tender shoots of the trees, vines, and
other things they planted were often cut off clean by the sharp
sand in the driving wind. They were surrounded by friendly
Indians who were willing to work and learn civilization, but
who were so hungry they could not resist the temptation to
pluck the young watermelons and squashes planted by the
missionaries, as fast as they approached the size of walnuts.
Once, when visiting the Muddy settlement of St. Joseph, the
Indian visitors were delighted with the rice my mother was
preparing to cook. They called it the "snow-white wheat" and
begged for some, saying they would plant and cultivate it with
great care. She humored them, but showed them how the

8

germ was destroyed, and advised them to cook it, and plant corn and melons.

In a brief time the Missionaries were short of the good things they had provided; there were no stores, freight trains seldom came that way, and they were a long distance, three day's travel from St. George, itself a pioneer settlement in an alkali desert. President Erastus Snow, with fatherly kindness, sent beef, cattle and flour to the Indians, to stay their increasing instincts for self-preservation by way of appropriation. Another misfortune befell the Missionaries; their dwellings were as dry as tinder, and in some way a fire started, and some lost their all, everyone lost something. President Erastus Snow called upon the people of St. George, and if I remember right, of Washington and Santa Clara also and with all possible haste sent the willing contributions of their brethren and sisters. President Brigham Young had two daughters, a son and a niece on the same mission. He visited them and was filled with compassion for their situation, and as it seemed vain to hope for an amelioration of some of their disadvantages, the Mission was broken up. Mrs. Felt's health was poor but, she says, "I never felt to murmur, but to stay as long as required." In 1869, Mrs. Felt went on a visit to her father in Connecticut, as he was not expected to live. He had gone back for the recovery of his health but was no better. She remained with him three months, then returned to Utah. In 1872 they moved to the Eleventh Ward, "and then," she says, "began some of the happiest days of my life. I soon became a member of the Y. L. M. I. A., and thereby received a better understanding of my religion, which brought me peace and happiness, such as I had never known before. I also became thoroughly convinced of the truth of the principle of celestial marriage, and having no children of my own was very desirous my husband should take other wives that he might have a posterity to do him honor, and after he took another wife and had children born to him, the Lord gave me a mother's love for them; they seemed as if they were indeed my own, and they seem to have the same love for me they do

for their own mother." I have witnessed the real mother in
this family, rocking her babe to sleep, and the other mother
—Louie—would sit beside her and hold one little hand, or
lay her own upon its little head, and it would quietly resign
itself to sleep, so closely were all these three true hearts united
in love. "In September, 1878, I was appointed to the position
of President of the P. A. of the Eleventh Ward, which
position I still hold.   In December of the same year. Mrs.
Freeze chose me as her First Counselor, in the stake organization of the Young Ladies' Association, and I immediately
started with President Freeze, visiting these wards, and I enjoyed my labor.   In September, 1879, I was appointed to fill
the position of Territorial President of the Primary Improvement Associations, and have visited the different stakes of Zion
as much as circumstances would permit, and now feel more
firm in my religion, and more determined to magnify my calling whereunto I have been appointed, hoping thereby to bring
honor to the cause of Zion and also to myself."

In person, Mrs. Felt is very tall and slender, her health
always being very delicate.   Her face is pale, refined and
spiritual in its expression; her spirit buoyant and cheerful,
and her animated manner and smile as frank as a child's; the
beholder would never take her for "a sorrowing Mormon
woman," such as we read about.   Whether presiding in gentle
dignity over a conference of several thousands of parents and
children, whether happily mingling in a reunion of cherished
and apppreciative friends, or whether in that closer, dearer
circle of which she is not the least the builder, her face is that
of innocence and purity; her heart is an altar to her God; her
life a monument to all.

ELLEN C. S. CLAWSON.

PRESIDENT OF THE PRIMARY ASSOCIATION OF THE SALT LAKE STAKE OF ZION.

Ellen Curtis Spencer Clawson was born in Saybrook, Conn., Nov. 1, 1832. She is the eldest daughter of Spencer Clawson, ✗ A. B., and Catherine Curtis, and grand daughter of Daniel Spencer, who fought in the Revolutionary War. Her father graduated at Union College, Schenectady, New York, and also at the Theological College at Hamilton, as a minister of the Baptist denomination. He received the gospel when his daughter was seven years old. He immediately sold his effects and went to Nauvoo, where he became intimately associated with the Prophet Joseph. At the age of nine years, she was baptized in the Mississippi river. During the exodus from Nauvoo her mother died from exposure and exhaustion, through leaving a comfortable house to camp out in mid-winter. Six months later her father was sent to Great Britain to take charge of the mission there. It was there he wrote the celebrated "Spencer's Letters," a little volume well known among the church works. He also became editor of the *Millennial Star*, which position he held for three years. He was obliged to leave his five remaining children in Ellen's care, she being now only thirteen years of age. During his absence the little family crossed the plains with ox teams, in President Brigham Young's company, taking five months to complete the journey, and suffering all the privations and hardships with the rest of the Saints.

Miss Ellen C. Spencer was married in March 1850, by President Brigham Young, to Hiram B. Clawson, who soon after became to President Young, business manager, a position he held for a number of years; subsequently superintendent of

✗ *Orson Spencer,*

the Z. C. M. I., and is at present Bishop of the Twelfth Ward, Salt Lake City. Mrs. Clawson is the mother of fourteen children, four sons and ten daughters, seven daughters and two sons of whom are now living. In April, 1879, Mrs Clawson was called to preside over the Primary Association of the Twelfth Ward, Salt Lake City, and later was ordained to preside over all the Primary Associations of the Salt Lake Stake of Zion.

Think of this noble girl, hardly more than a child, taking upon her young life the duties and cares of a loved and lost, a martyred mother! Surely she was precious in God's sight; and his arm must have sustained her through that long and lonely journey through the wilderness. That same strength of character, that same sweet patience of spirit, gentle manner, have upborne her through later eventful periods. A prominent and beautiful feature in her life, one that has won to her the truest respect, the unperishable love of her friends is the position she has maintained amid her husband's family, like a loving queen mother, in his home circle.

Mrs. Clawson's two sons, H. B. and Spencer Clawson, are in the mercantile business, the latter a wholesale merchant, both men of high social and business standing, and an honor to their parents.

EMELINE B. WELLS.

EDITOR OF "WOMAN'S EXPONENT."

This lady, like most of our representative women, was born in New England, February 29, 1828, at Petersham, Worcester County, Massachusetts. Her maiden name was Woodward. The forefathers of her family came in 1830, settled in and around Boston, were large landowners, and by profession were mathematicians, surveyors, etc. Mrs. Wells' ancestry, both on the father and mother's side, were purely of English extraction, and fought for freedom in the Revolutionary War, as well as that of 1812, some of them being officers of high rank. Her brothers and other relations fought in the late Civil War also. Mrs. Wells has had an eventful history in many respects, and somewhat romantic; were it to be published as a story and strictly true, it would be stranger than fiction.

In her early life she gave promise of unusual talent, her memory was quite wonderful, storing up the many incidents and points of beauty around her to be brought forth in after years in faithful portraiture amid far off valleys and places then unbuilt and undiscovered. It was the expectation of her family and friends that she would make a mark in the world and do them honor; this was to be verified, but in a way undreamed of by them. The place and work God had chosen for her had not in her childhood, even a name. The child of destiny, straying alone yet not lonely, with her busy fancies finding companionship in fields, woods and brooks, the haunts of nature in their rudest, wildest form; listening to the songs of birds and sighing of the forest leaves, touching with caressing hand the flowers and moss-grown rocks, searching through shrubbery and tangled vines, or looking up through alcoves green and dim, feasted her eyes upon the wondrous sky where moving clouds passed on in endless changes 'neath that world, where she was taught the home and throne of God forever are. These surroundings and influences developed and moulded that individuality of character during her childhood to the degree, that at eight years of age she commenced composing in rhyme, choosing instinctively the beautiful and harmonious method of expression which is poetry. This element cannot be possessed by anyone, old or young, but that it casts an influence recognized at once, and men and women gray haired now, say, that watching the thoughtful child they knew there was a special destiny for her, undefined, but nevertheless felt as something grand and great. So, hovered the spirit of her mission around her through her childhood, and at ten years of age she became a member of the church choir, happy in lifting her full heart in hymns of worship and of praise.

How many have found sweet joy in singing; that expression of supplication, faith and gratitude, which in any and every religion is, we feel, true and acceptable adoration.

In November, 1841, the Gospel was preached in her native village; and her mother believed and was baptized. Immediately a branch of the Church was organized and some excitement in regard to Mormonism sprang up among the worldly-wise and learned. Mrs. Wells' mother persuaded her to go and hear the Mormon elders, and told her she knew it was the true Gospel that the ancient Apostles taught, and that she had been looking forward to such a dispensation. She was a woman of very strong mind, of practical capabilities, yet withal very spiritual in her nature, had been for many years a staunch Congregationalist, and had her children brought up in that church. Ministers, lawyers, judges and influential men came with their profound learning and logic to convince Mrs. Wells' mother that Mormonism was a delusion, but all in vain. On the young and inexperienced daughter they expected to be able to make an impression, and no means was left untried. Everything that could be said or done was brought to bear, and when she had decided to receive the ordinance of baptism all the powers of darkness seemed to conspire to hinder it. She affirms that a power she had no knowledge of heretofore, seemed to possess her at this moment-ous time to help her to withstand the intercessions and plead-ings of those who had been her friends, and who now so vigorously sought to keep her from going down into the waters of baptism.

On the 1st day of March, 1842, when a little group of Latter-Day Saints was assembled to perform the ordinance of baptism on her mother's own ground, just near her home, zealous friends sent messengers down to ask her if she was *sure* she was acting of her own free will and choice, otherwise they would take her by force and she should never lack for means of a higher education, but if she accepted the Mormon faith and gathered at Nauvoo she *must* renounce not only her friends but also all the advantages of literary culture she had so ardently hoped to attain, and be forever disgraced. Not knowing but that it was true that her hopes for further advancement must be resigned, she laid them on the altar of her faith, willing to yield up her future entirely to the will and care of her Creator. Some power potent indeed buoyed her up and she went through this trying ordeal and though her delicate nerves were somewhat shaken yet she told her mother and friends then what proved true afterwards, that the crisis was past, she had renounced all she had before looked forward to, henceforth she desired to dedicate herself entirely to the work in which she had enlisted.

During the year after her coming into the Church she pur-sued her studies at the same school, yet she had to endure a great deal of ridicule on account of being a Mormon, and her teacher never wearied of persuading and entreating her to give up such foolish ideas, and resume her place among her asso-ciates. But though she was as one alone, for there was not another in the school that believed in the peculiar faith she had embraced, and she understood very little herself, still she had an innate conception of the entire consecration necessary for a Latter-Day Saint. The next year she taught a country school, receiving her certificate as readily as any of the other young ladies; and early in the spring of 1844, in the month of April, she went up to Nauvoo, where she had the privilege of hearing Joseph Smith preach his last discourses. After reaching Nauvoo she received strong testimony, not by any spiritual manifestations, but that which convinced her reason and intelligence.

We cannot attempt to give in detail the changes and trials of Nauvoo, but suffice it to say that through sickness, sorrow and severe trial she kept the faith.

In the winter of 1844-45, she was taught the principle of celestial marriage by Bishop Newel K. Whitney and his wife, whose acquaintance she had formed through having been introduced to the family by a cousin of Sister Whitney's. This cousin was one of the company in which she had traveled to Nauvoo, and who because of her delicate health, her youth and inexperience, had been attracted towards her.

She accepted the principle in its sacred phase and entered into the order or covenant of celestial marriage with the same purity of motive that had influenced her in going down into the waters of baptism. The ceremony was performed by Brigham Young in one of the upper rooms of the Bishop's house in Nauvoo, in the evening of the 14th day of February, 1845, the only witness being the Bishop's first wife, who not only had consented but actually urged the matter, and gave her to her husband; and the most sincere friendship existed forever afterward between the two, who really lived like mother and daughter, and though so intimately associated in the same family, and sometimes under circumstances the most trying, yet no jar or contention ever marred their true friendship for each other. To those who doubt the fact of women living happily together no better illustration can be given than such practical ones as these. Here were two refined, sensitive natures in harmony with that condition of marriage, but it was from the fact that they accepted it from divine authority as a part of their religion, and a higher law which would secure to them a future exaltation; never losing sight of the exalted nature of their mission, having undertaken

8

to live lives of self-sacrifice and purity. The false assertion made by the world that women of marked character and attainments would never submit to live in the order of plural marriage is disproved by such instances as this one. Both were women of high social attainments, and possessing superior qualities of mind and heart.

It is the higher nature that must be aroused to inspire women to carry out practically this exalting, refining principle, and through this crucible many have come forth like gold seven times purified, tried as by fire yet without the smell upon their garments.

Mrs. Wells received the ordinances and the blessings of the Temple with her husband in Nauvoo, and came out in the month of February, crossing the Mississippi River on the ice. Her mother, who had been a staunch Latter-Day Saint from her first hearing the Gospel preached, died of hardships and fatigue when the Saints were driven from Nauvoo.

In Winter Quarters she taught school and came with the Bishop and his family to the valley, leaving the Missouri River towards the last of May, 1845, and arrived in the valley early in October. On the 2nd day of November, after, her eldest daughter was born in a wagon, during one of those cold piercing wind and sleet storms that often occur at that season. September 23, 1850, Bishop Whitney died, leaving her a widow at twenty-two with two children, the eldest not then two years of age, the youngest a babe five weeks old. Many of her friends feared she would sink beneath her trials, but she rallied those forces of her nature, which under a husband's care had never been called into requisition, and turned to the ways and means of providing for her little ones. Left as it were alone, bereft and so helpless, the young mother was like one in a dream, she had trusted to her husband so entirely, and knew so little herself of the practical realities of life; she had not thought he could die. He was one to lean upon, and she had looked up to him as a little child looks up to a true loving parent with a reverence almost more than human. To her he had shown the utmost tenderness, helping and encouraging in

times of severe trial, making every burden lighter because of
the intense sympathy of his spiritual nature. This was one of
the eventful epochs of her life. She awakened to know that
for her, duty must be first, and she became in course of time
accustomed to acting for herself instead of leaning upon
another.

It was a hard lesson, but she studied it carefully, and sought
earnestly for divine help upon her efforts; but we are simply
giving a few facts and not minute details, therefore suffice it
to say after something more than two years of widowhood she
married again.

During the Bishop's life, he frequently prophesied to her of
the future and what her work would yet be, and although she
could not then imagine how such changes could possibly be
wrought, (as much on account of the condition of the country
and the circumstances of the people,) yet looking back over it
now, she realizes how prophetic his words were, and the
promises made concerning her future have many of them been
fulfilled.

Mrs. Wells often says she was born a womans' rights advocate, inheriting it from her mother, who was a staunch advocate
for woman's emancipation, and when left a widow with a large
family, realized more fully the injustice of the laws in regard
to women, their property rights and guardianship of children.
Mrs. Wells has been the mother of six children, one son and
five daughters, and during their childhood devoted herself
almost exclusively to their care and education.

Mrs. Wells has always had a great desire to see others advance, and in her home before she entered upon public duties
ever sought to stimulate those around her to efforts of development of the higher nature. She has given much genuine
encouragement to those who would shrink from criticism and
would consequently, unless aroused, bury their talents or fold
them away in a napkin. She is exceedingly frank in her
nature and generous to a fault, and possesses an admirable
faculty of entertaining those with whom she is from time to
time associated. She has drawn around her people of taste,

ability and culture; the secret of her winning friends is perhaps in her almost total forgetfulness of self, and her intense
wish to make others happy. Perhaps, among her friends,
few are fonder or more sincere than those who have received
both sympathy, encouragement and advice from her who has
not feared that other lights might dim her own, she has rejoiced
in the progress and victories of others as though they were her
own achievements.

It is truly wonderful to contemplate the public work accomplished by Mrs. Wells in the comparatively brief opportunity
of time since her labors began. In the Eastern States
prominent women have pursued these objects for nearly fifty
years, but the women of Utah have stood afar and alone with
no part in matters of a political nature until about thirteen
years ago. They have exercised their privileges with respect,
caution and wisdom, holding neither lightly or boastfully the
freedom of the ballot. Many have read law and studied par-
liamentary rules, and have on occasions of public character
endeavored to profit by observation in the presentation and
discussion of such matters.

Mrs. Wells has traveled much among our people, speaking
and assisting in organizing. She has good executive ability
and is well adapted to this kind of work.

In political matters she takes great interest, and since the
women of Utah have had the ballot she has taken a prominent
part in that direction and done much active work.

Mrs. Wells went to Washington as a delegate from the
women of Utah in January, 1879, to attend the Convention of
the National Woman Suffrage Association, accompanied by
Mrs. Zina Young Williams and while there they had the
opportunity of speaking before committees of House and Sen-
ate, and also had an audience with President Hayes and
several of the leading men of the nation on the Mormon
question. They also prepared a memorial to Congress and
succeeded in getting it presented.

In November, 1874, Mrs. Wells went into the office of the
Woman's Exponent to assist the editor, Mrs. Lula Greene

Richards, a little in her labors, and gradually grew interested
in the work, and in May, 1875, her labors became regular and
constant, continuing so until in July, 1877, when she assumed
the entire responsibility, Mrs. Richards withdrawing on account of increased domestic cares. Mrs. Wells never seems
to tire of journalistic duty.

In November, 1876, she was chosen President of the Central
Grain Committee for the storing of grain by women, against a
day of famine. At the Mass Meeting in the Theatre to protest
against the Woman's Anti-Polygamic Association she took an
active part in the proceedings. In September, 1882, Mrs.
Wells went to Omaha with Mrs. Zina D. H. Young, to attend
the convention of the National Womans' Suffrage Association
again. Mrs. Wells was appointed Secretary of the Deseret
Hospital Association; in fact her time is almost constantly
employed in the performance of public duties and benevolent
work.

Looking retrospectively upon the life of Emmeline B. Wells
and noting the constant upward progress she has made through
the adverse circumstances common to a pioneer life, and the
establishing of a new order of religion and social life amid the
opposition and persecution of our own nation; the result is
calculated to testify strongly against the assertions made that,
in our isolation and subservience to religious authority, woman
is repressed in her abilities and privileges; for it is in that
mental atmosphere which is the very essence of Mormonism,
that her's have been developed and brought into prominence
as an exemplar to the young. If in the very stronghold of
Mormonism the standard of progress is upheld by woman's
hand as well as man's, the inference is that the next generation
will show a marked advance. Knowledge is power, and this
with virtue and wisdom united, guided by inspiration, ignorance
and tyranny will alike be impotent against the growing hosts
of Israel. And, knowing this, all excellences of acquirements
and attainments are stimulated and promoted among the old
and young by our leaders, misrepresentation to the contrary
notwithstanding.

The quality of statesmanship is of high order and rare among women, but it has been declared by the lips of prophecy that positions of power would await the women of Zion faster than they would be qualified for them. Mrs. Wells is by nature one of those prepared for the advent of such an era.

And still, the songs whispered from nature to the heart of the child chime on, and the woman repeats them in clear, sweet utterances to the world; the intuitions of the Deity and his work she may now declare in knowledge, and the maiden that with timid feet went down at the Gospel's call into the waters of baptism, has become a strength, an inspiration and a guide to women in the same path.

President Young gave Mrs. Wells a mission to record in brief the biographies of the most prominent women of our Church, in the *Woman's Exponent*. A part of this work has already been performed, which is an important addition to our home literature.

I give below one selection from the lady's many beautiful poems:

REAL AND IDEAL.

At times, sweet visions float across my mind,
    And glimpses of the unknown bright and fair,
Where all the objects seem so well defined—
    Tasteful in color, and in beauty rare,
That I must pause and think if they be real,
Or only what the poets call ideal.

I well remember when a little child,
    I had these same strange, wand'ring fancies;
And I was told my thoughts were running wild,
    That I must not indulge in such romances.
Wasting in idle dreams the precious hours,
Building air castles and gazing from the towers.

E'en then I seemed to see familiar friends,
    Pertaining to a dim, uncertain past;
And to my recollection faintly clings,
    A sense of something which the shadows cast,
That showed me what my future life would be,
A prophecy, as 'twere, of destiny.

There was an intuition in my heart,
  An innate consciousness of right and wrong,
That bade me choose a wiser, better part,
  Which, in rough places helped to make me strong:
And though my path was oft bereft of beauty,
Still urged me on to fulfill ev'ry duty.

O, happy childhood, bright with faith and hope;
  Enchantment dwells within thy rosy bowers,
And rainbow tints gild all within thy scope;
  And youth sits lightly on a bed of flowers,
His cup of happiness just brimming o'er,
Unconscious of what life has yet in store.

What glowing aspirations fill the mind—
Of noble work designed for man to do!
What purity of purpose here we find—
  What longing for the beautiful and true;
Ere know we of the toil, and grief and woe;
Or dream that men and women suffer so.

Though all along life's toilsome, weary way,
  We meet with disappointments hard to bear;
Yet strength is given equal to our day,
  And joy is ofnest mixed with pain or care;
But let us not grow weary in well-doing,
Still persevere, the upward path pursuing.

Thus ever struggle on, 'mid doubts and fears;
  While changing scenes before our gaze unfold,
Till, through the vista of long weary years,
  We see Heaven's sunshine thro' its gates of gold;
And feel assured it is an answering token,
Aye! though our earthly idols have been broken.

Tho' those we've cherished most have been untrue,
  And fond and faithful ones have gone before,
Still let us keep the promises in view,
  Of those who're pleading on " the other shore, "
Whose tender messages are with us yet,
The words of love, we never can forget.

And while we muse and ponder, shadows fall,
  And a sweet spirit whispers, "Peace, be still;"
What of the past—'tis now beyond recall:
  The future, we with usefulness may fill.
Yet sometime we shall find in regions real
Those dreams fulfilled we only term ideal.

MRS. ROMANIA B. PRATT, M. D.

Romania Bunnell Pratt, daughter of Luther B. and Esther Mendenhall Bunnell, was born August 8, 1839, in Washington, Wayne County, Indiana. In her seventh year she went with her parents to Nauvoo, and had the privilege of visiting the Temple, and went with the Church to Winter Quarters. She says: "While there I well remember being present when the martial band was marching round and the call was made for the Mormon Batallion for Mexico. Although too young to appreciate the severe ordeal our devoted and persecuted people were subject to, I can never forget the feeling of grief which oppressed my little heart, as one after one the brave-hearted men fell into the ranks." From Winter Quarters her parents moved to Ohio where her whole time was spent in attending school, the last year and a half at the Crawfordsville Female Seminary. In 1855, her mother then being a widow, with her family of two girls and two boys and their worldly effects, again joined the Saints at Atchison, now Omaha, where she was first baptized into the Church of Jesus Christ of Latter-Day Saints, on the last of May, 1855, just before commencing their journey with ox teams across the plains to Salt Lake City, where they arrived September 3d of the same year. The summer journey of these months was a series of changing panoramic scenes as enchanting to the free, careless heart of a child, as it was arduous to those of maturer years. Their arrival in the city of the Saints was during the grasshopper famine, when flour was twenty-five dollars per hundred weight, sugar forty cents per pound and everything in proportion, and although they had left plenty behind them, in the hands of guardians who refused to allow them any money, (the children all being minors) to come away among the Mormons, saying; "They will rob you of it all as soon as you get there. " In consequence of this predjudice they arrived in Salt Lake City penniless and at a time when they with thousands of others had to learn the sweetness of the coarsest kind of bread. Romania taught day school and gave music lessons on the piano at intervals until she entered the medical profession. This lady was married to Parley P. Pratt, son of the Apostle, Parley P. Pratt, by President Brigham Young, and has had seven children; Parley P. Pratt, Luther B., Louis L., Corinne T., Mark C., Irwin E. and Roy B. Pratt. Her second son died in infancy, and her lovely daughter died when twenty months old.

Through a love of literary pursuit and surrounding circumstances her attention was turned to the medical profession which she entered in 1873 and graduated in the Woman's Medical College of Philadelphia in March, 1877. After graduating she remained in Philadelphia and took special courses on the eye and ear at Wills' Hospital and a dispensary on Chestnut Street, conducted by Dr. George Strawbridge. Leaving Philadelphia she spent a few weeks visiting Hydropathic institutions to learn something of the mode of administration and especially of water treatment.

Immediately on her arrival home she by request commenced giving lectures to ladies and agitated the question of a hospital for women and children, and by counsel on account of great demand of obstetrical aid needed in the numerous settlements, soon instituted a school of midwifery, and has taught two classes a year since, except when absent for special study in the New York Eye and Ear Infirmary where she spent eight months in 1881-2.

In 1874, when Eliza R. S. Smith organized the Young Ladies' Mutual Improvement Association of the Twelfth Ward, Mrs. Pratt was appointed President, which position she held though absent a portion of the time, until professional work compelled her resignation. She now holds the office of Treasurer of the Salt Lake Stake organization of the Young Ladies Mutual Improvement Association, and is also one of the Board of Executors and medical attendant of the Deseret

10

Hospital, organized 1882, beside having a busy practice. Luther B. Bunnell, her father, was the inventor of a repeating fire arm, and at a critical period in the persecutions of the Saints, donated to them five hundred dollars in arms and ammunition. Tracing her family record a few years back, we find in her mother's line the names of Bayard Taylor and Benjamin West among her relatives. About the year 1837, a small pamphlet was published in Philadelphia giving the geneaology of her family, tracing them back to a Russian nobleman. Captain Mendenhall was the grandson of Benjamin, brother to John Mendenhall, the Puritan emigrant. Colonel Richard Thomas, brother to her great grandmother, was a member of Congress from Chester County, Pa., for many years. Of medical members, Dr. Pratt's family certainly has had a goodly number, and of these we select—Dr. Mendenhall, of Richmond, Indiana, her mother's cousin, Dr. Marmaduke Mendenhall, of North Carolina, her cousin, Dr. Paris Mendenhall, her brother, Dr. James R. Mendenhall, of, Richmond, Indiana, her cousin, Nereus Mendenhall, professor in New Garden Quaker College, also George D. and William Mendenhall, physicians. Beside these, many others of note occur, too many for less than a special volume. Her eldest son, Parley P. Pratt, also entered the New York School of Pharmacy, from which he expects to graduate in the spring of 1885.

Dr. Pratt is in appearance the very embodiment of health and happiness, her blooming cheeks, abundant loose ringlets without a line of gray, her dark eyes inspiring the dispirited with cheerfulness and hope, the cordial clasp of hand, a hand gentle, but somehow suggestive of the nerve, firmness, self-possession and power the true healer holds, the intuition one receives of her sympathy and benevolence, if needed; all these are conveyed as upon an open page by the very presence of Dr. Pratt. Also, that other influence is felt that she too leans upon a higher power than human skill, the same Giver of life and health as the tenderest child looks up to.

Dr. Romania B. Pratt was the first "Mormon" woman graduate. Following her return as graduate, next came Dr.

Ellis R. Shipp, 1878, Mattie Paul Hughes, M. D., 1883, Elvira S. Barney, M. D., 1883, and Margaret C. Shipp, M. D., 1883. Drs. R. B. Pratt, Ellis R. Shipp and Elvira S. Barney are connected with the Deseret Hospital, founded in 1882.

THE LADY DOCTOR.

For her, from darkened rooms
  What blessings softly rise,
Who brings relief to pain and fear
  And soothes the watcher's cries.

On her, the skies look down
  As fearless, swift she goes
Through lonely paths, past rude alarms,
  And oft through blinding snows.

'Tis hers, to see the smile
  The new blest mother gives ;
And hers to hear their answering joy—
  "Hush all thy fears, he lives."

The record of her works
  In volumes ne'er is known,
'Tis written as on marble carved
  In grateful hearts alone.

DR. ELVIRA S. BARNEY.

Although in this book Dr. Barney is classed among the medical fraternity her labors and history have been interwoven with those of the Latter Day Saints from her childhood, in so many varied and useful fields of labor, that I am compelled to pause at the very beginning of this sketch, (necessarily brief) knowing I must omit so many particulars, both valuable and instructive.

If Dr. Barney had, in her childhood, possessed the advantages of obtaining a thorough education, and opportunities for the best development of those many abilities which have manifested themselves under the most dispiriting surroundings, it would be difficult at present to estimate what she might have accomplished. She represents the practical, domestic, experience of a Latter Day Saint; orphaned, and almost alone, but possessing that indomitable spirit that rises above every obstacle, and turns to account every available means no matter how humble, that cultivates every inherent power to its best uses; an upbuilder in everything pertaining to the interests of her people, ready to aid on the right and on the left, forgetful of self.

Elvira S. Barney was born March 17, 1832, in Gerry, Chawtawque County, New York, being the daughter of Samuel C. Stevens, a merchant, and his wife, Minerva Althea Field, a school teacher. Her great grand-father, Joseph Stevens, took an active part in the Revolutionary War; her grand-father, Simon Stevens, was a doctor; her uncles were doctors and lawyers. When twelve years old Elvira heard the gospel preached by a Mormon Elder, and from that time daily prayed in secret till the Lord gave her a testimony that satisfied her heart.

She was baptized in 1844, and went with her parents to Nauvoo, where her father died after a brief illness, on October 4th. In the January following Elvira and her mother were preparing for the journey across the wilderness, parching corn, etc.; but her mother, overcome by toil, grief and exhaustion, died on the 6th of the month. Their farm, household goods, etc., were sold, and the five children received ten dollars each to fit them out for a western journey. Elvira parted with her twin brother, fourteen years old, with tears in his eyes, and she never saw him again. He died six years after. Elvira was taken some twenty-five miles across the prairie among strangers, and there spent the winter. There were no children for her to mate with, no one to feel tenderly for the lonely, quiet aching heart of this orphan girl. When spring approached she rejoined her married sister to wait upon her, traveling west with her, sometimes living in a brush-house (while recruiting) and sleeping under a wagon while traveling, and once awoke to find several inches of snow covering them. Exposure brought her to death's door, but she lived after long suffering. She witnessed the solemn separation of the "Mor-Battallion" from their families and friends. During one winter she lived in a dug-out in a side hill on the Missouri River, and was forced to live on corn bread and water; their tallow candles they could not afford to burn, but used them to grease their bake-kettles. Here, however, willing to be useful she helped to teach school, studying nights by a chip-fire to keep in advance of her pupils. Many of our public speakers of to-day, can date their first lessons in elocution and arithmetic to her training.

Elvira crossed the mountains in the first company in 1848, and arrived in this valley by the side of two yoke of oxen, with a sick sister and a brother-in-law with a broken arm, in her care. Her first lesson in surgery was the helping to set this arm, and her first practice in medicine was the breaking up of her sister's fever. Soon after this Elvira made herself a pair of buck-skin moccasins. The first meeting she attended was in a bowery, and her best calico dress had patches on the elbows. Before the next winter she worked six weeks for a pair of leather shoes. There was not much aristocracy here in those days. They held meetings in tents, sang praises to God, and danced with as much sincerity and purity of heart as even King David did before the Lord, for they knew God was with them. Said her sister, who afterward turned from the faith: "If God had not been with us when we were driven out at the battle of Nauvoo, we should have perished, but when we were starving he sent quails, and they were so tame they came into our tents where the sick were lying, and they even took them in their hands." Thousands witnessed the miracle. After they arrived in the valley, crickets large and numerous threatened their crops, (their only recourse) but the Lord in answer to prayers sent sea-gulls in such flocks that the air was darkened, and they destroyed the crickets. The heavens were not as brass above their heads; they helped and loved each other, and God heard and loved them. Their laws were few and simple; in a Bishop's court a brother forgave his brother.

In the summer of 1849, Elvira earned fifty dollars at different kinds of work, and making straw hats for the emigrants going to California to get gold the Battallion boys were the first to find. In the spring of 1849, Elvira had been appointed to go on a mission to the Society Islands; this was postponed, and in the spring of 1851, with her husband, she started in the company of Apostle Parley P. Pratt on his mission to Chili. They were harrassed by Indians while crossing the deserts, and Elvira arrived in Los Angelos sick with a fever, and laid sixteen days in a tent made of sheets. Her sister here buried her babe; took steamer and landed in San Francisco, Elvira contracting inflamatory rheumatism on the voyage, and was stiff and helpless four days. Parley P. Pratt administered to her, and the next morning she helped to get breakfast. Through some trouble between the Islanders and the French the Mission was changed to the Sandwich Islands. Having been left behind to recruit her health, Sister Elvira went to work in a hotel as waiter at one hundred dollars a month, and

soon was able to pay her passage to the Sandwich Islands, besides having means to support her while there.   On arriving
at Lahaiva, on the island of Mai, the captain gave her his arm
and they walked through the streets in quest of her husband
followed by the natives, old and young, they to admire and be
friendly, the strangers feeling mortified with such honors.
Remained a month there then embarked on the ship Hulu-
mann. The previously mentioned captain came on board and
treated them to a Christmas dinner.   After four days sail
landed at Kawhow, Hwaii, in the fall of 1851.   Sister Elvira
lived six months among the natives on their island food,
mostly of taro and sweet-potatoes made into a batter and
soured, short rations at that, yet attained the weight of one
hundred and fifty pounds. Says she: "Don't smile when I
tell you I often thought of Alexander Selkirk who said he was
'Monarch of all he surveyed.' Here months passed, living on
the lava strewn island, no ships came to bring tidings, I was
left to view the rolling billows that separated me from all I held
dear, country and friends. Fancy the loneliness of those long
months, not a white woman to speak to in my own tongue.
Here I was studying a foreign language and teaching the natives to speak my own." In the mean time sister Elvira acquired the art of swimming, which means enabled her afterwards,to all appearances, to save one of the ladies of this book
from drowning in a bottomless spring in Utah.   During eleven
months spent on four islands, Sister Elvira wrote a letter to a
native lawyer in his own tongue, and although over thirty
years have elapsed she is able to converse fluently with the natives who have gathered to this city.

Leaving all her means but five dollars with her husband,
she arrived penniless at Honolulu *en route* for San Francisco,
by counsel of Phillip B. Lewis, President of the Sandwich
Islands Mission. Here, in answer to prayer, after all other
efforts had failed to procure means, a stranger she never saw
before nor since, called upon her. In answer to his few questions he learned her situation as a missionary's wife preaching
the Gospel without purse or scrip. He handed her the money,

eighty dollars, to pay her passage to San Francisco, and she gave him her note for it, and embarked. Three times she escaped shipwreck, the last time, just outside the Golden Gate of the Bay of San Francisco. On her arrival there she borrowed the money of a friend and returned it to the stranger, and repaid this by making fine shirts at ten dollars apiece. The wife of the gentleman for whom she made them presented her with a complete set of clothing, the outer garment being a new silk dress. Sister Elvira says: "The Lord knew I needed them and I thanked Him and the giver also." Of the San Francisco Saints she says, "The welcome I received by the remaining Saints there, and the heavenly influence we enjoyed together is the one most marked oasis of my life, for truly they blessed me and God blessed them." Sister Elvira wasted no time, but in various ways earned means, part of which she sent to assist the Sandwich Islands Mission. In 1856 she returned to Salt Lake City, riding seven hundred miles on horseback, and here resumed school teaching. In 1859, she assisted in the amputation of a dear friend's arm. In 1860, traveled east to visit kindred and rode sixteen days by stage. In 1864, went to Wheaton College and returned home after nearly two years absence. From 1859 to 1863 had taught school in ten different places, generally four terms a year. Had during these previous years taken at different times four homeless children into her care until other ways opened for them. In 1873 adopted a boy whom she schooled and provided for for ten years. In this year also began writing up her genealogical record which she has traced back to the year 1600. In 1876 wrote a pamphlet on seri-culture, and suggested the appointment of a meeting on that subject. Advanced as a loan the first fifty dollars to establish the "home made straw hat industry." Canvassed the Thirteenth Ward and traveled in the interest of the *Woman's Exponent*. Was appointed agent for and canvassed the city for the *Women of Mormondom*, and raised fifty shares ($25.00 each) in one day. Was appointed a committee for purchasing grain for the Grain Association (President E. B. Wells). In 1876 traveled south and held forty-five meetings in twenty-seven days, in the interest of Women's Work in Utah. In 1878 attended the Deseret University. Up to date of February, 1879, had earned over nine thousand dollars by her own labors, and built a good commodious house, her home. October, 1879, started East to continue her medical studies which she had prosecuted at home for several years, and attended three complete courses; returning home in the spring of 1883, prepared to pursue this her chosen vocation after a long and eventful experience in many fields of usefulness.

Realizing her own early desires for knowledge and the inconvenience of limited privileges, Dr. Barney fitted up her large house to accommodate lady boarders,thus affording them the convenience of home and college under one roof, with the privilege of boarding themselves, and receiving gratuitous medical instructions for one year.

She has crossed the Pacific Ocean twice, the western deserts twice, the eastern plains five times: has wrought at different humble occupations belonging to a new country, learning later fine embroidery, pencil work, draughting in architecture, delivering lectures, &c., one tenth cannot be told in these pages. Sister Barney also has received the gifts of prophecy, tongues and interpretation of tongues, as the writer can testify.

Her step is as quick as ever, her carriage erect; she says; " My life has been real, my life has been earnest, and now if any of my works praise me then truly I am praised. If any one has done better I should be happy to read their chapter; yet I realize many of our Mormon ladies lives have been similar, and it is such women that will teach and train sons for the nation. "

11

EMILY HILL WOODMANSEE.

Emily Hill Woodmansee, daughter of Thomas and Elizabeth Slade Hill, was born in the south-west of England, near Warminster, Wilts, March 24, 1836. Quoting her own words:

"Of my pedigree I will simply say that my parents were honorable, hard-working people, too independent in spirit to stoop to mean actions, much less to sully their conscience to curry favor. The youngest living of eleven children, I fully enjoyed the privileges often accorded the youngest member of a family, (i e) of having things my own way. My parents as well as my brothers and sisters were very kind to me, and I can truly say—slightly reversing a word in the lines of one of our poets, that,

'I never knew what trouble was
Till I became a Mormon.'

" When but a mere child I was much concerned about my eternal salvation and felt that I would make any sacrifice to obtain it. I asked all kinds of questions of my mother and sisters, seeking how to be saved, but could get no satisfaction from them nor from the religious body (Wesleyans) to which they belonged.

Hungry and thirsty for truth, I searched the Scriptures, invariably turning to the lives of ancient apostles or to the beautiful writings of the Prophet Isaiah. I was never weary of reading his prophecies, the glory of a Latter-Day Zion that burthened his inspirations possessed for me a charm irresistible. Truly I was waiting for something, I knew not what, that came to me sooner than I expected.

" When I was about twelve years old, my cousin, Miriam Slade, (afterward the wife of Edward Hanham,) came to visit us; she was very merry-hearted and we had anticipated her visit, expecting a good deal of fun; but she was too full of a 'new religion' to do anything but preach. 'God,' she said, 'had spoken from the heavens to a man named Joseph Smith; the Gospel was restored to the earth, the honest in heart were commanded to gather to the land of Zion for safety, for this was the last Dispensation, and the hour of God's judgment had come!'

"Right faithfully she testified to her knowledge of these things, much to the surprise of our family, who were considerably amused at her earnestness as well as at the novelty of her belief, and notwithstanding I listened attentively, I thought her assertions too good to be true. The next Sunday my cousin informed us that the Latter-Day Saints had appointed a meeting for that day at an adjoining village called Chalford, and invited us to go. As it was a distance of five or six miles, making a long walk there and back, none of my brothers cared to go, and my elder sisters considered themselves altogether too respectable (?) to attend an outdoor meeting of such a primitive sect, therefore they declined to go, and no one thought of sending me till I suggested it. Turning to my father, my sisters said, (laughingly,) 'Yes, send Em, she will tell us all about it.'

"In five minutes Miriam Slade and myself were on the road, accompanied by Mr. Wm. Bowring, (brother to Henry E. Bowring of Brigham City,) and by Edward W. Tullidge, then a youth, but now well-known as a talented writer and also as the proprietor and editor of *Tullidge's Quarterly Magazine.* Never, never shall I forget that day, surely it was the turning point of my whole life. A few devoted worshippers of truth met together in a small house, to bear their testimony to one another and to worship God! And He was in their midst and that to bless them. Even as in the Day of Pentecost, they spake in tongues and prophesied, which prophecy I have seen fulfilled. Unlike the Jews who were 'pricked in their hearts,' I did not even ask, 'What shall I do to be saved.' 'The way' was open before me, and simple and young as I was I instinctively knew that 'I could not err therein.'

The Eternal! spake, and honest hearts discerning
The voice and message of the holiest One!
Hail it as though their souls had e'en been yearning
For light and truth, e'en since their lives begun.

"It was indeed as though I had been brought 'out of darkness into marvelous light,' and I could not shut my eyes against it.

"In the evening I attended an out door 'Mormon Meeting,' and though naturally sensitive to ridicule, I did not care the least for the sneers of the crowd but joined in the songs of the Saints as well as I could, for in my childish way I wanted it understood that I was not ashamed to count one with the peculiar people called Latter-Day Saints.

"Many a time since, when 'offences' have come in my way, over which with mortal weakness I have almost stumbled, the testimony of that eventful day has been to me a precious recollection which nothing could obliterate. I was so overjoyed at finding what I had so long desired, and so eager to convince my friends that I could hardly wait to get home. As soon as I was inside the house and almost before anyone else could speak ,I astounded them all by the emphatic declaration that I knew the Latter-Day Saints were the right people; and I would join them as soon as I was big enough. I was never sent to 'take notes' of the 'Mormons' again, but on the contrary was closely watched lest I should be led away by a 'sect that was everywhere spoken against.' My early study of the Scriptures now stood me in good stead, and I searched the Bible more diligently than ever, so that I might give a good reason for my faith to the hosts that assailed me, (right reverends among the number,) who, finding it easier to cry 'delusion' than to prove it, generally wound up by informing me that I wasn't old enough to know my own mind, and was altogether too young to judge of so grave a matter. Meantime my persistent faith invoked such a tempest of wrath over my head, that I could not even get an opportunity to be baptized, and the elders did not think it wisdom (because of my tender years) to perform the ceremony without my parents' consent. I well remember looking forward to a period when I should be old enough to act for myself, and it seemed a lifetime.

" About this time one of the elders brought Brother John Halliday (brother to Bishop Halliday of Santaquin) to our house, who bore such a powerful testimony to the divine mission of Joseph Smith, that my sister, Julia, (now Mrs. Ivins of St. George) exclaimed, 'If ever there was a man of God I'm sure he is one, and I'll be a Latter-Day Saint, too!' From that time I had a friend in the family, and we were both determined that cost what it might we would be true to the light within us. Only once in a great while could we steal away and meet with the Saints, but although we were not yet baptized we partook of the sacrament and paid out our pocket money to the Church funds like actual members.

"On one of these occasions Brother Halliday blessed me and confirmed upon me the promise that I should write in prose and in verse and thereby comfort the hearts of thousands. After this I was baptized March 25, 1858, I was then sixteen, but had virtually been a Latter-Day Saint for four years. .

" Denied the privilege of freely meeting with the Saints, I all the more earnestly desired to gather to Zion; but fearing I might be forcibly detained if I attempted to leave home directly for America, I obtained my parents' consent to visit my sister, Julia—who had already gone to Northampton (quite a long distance from home) hoping that the way would open up, so we might earn enough to emigrate. There for the first time I enjoyed religious freedom and there also I took my lessons of hard times; preparing me for greater hardships in store.

"In the month of May, 1856, we sailed for America on the ship, *Thornton*, Captain Collins, commander; Brother James G. Willie had charge of the Saints, (a company of eight hundred) and a good captain he was. We had a pleasant trip with the exception of one heavy storm which I would not have missed for a great deal.

"From New York we traveled by rail and by way of Lake Erie to the camping ground in the neighborhood of Iowa City; there we were obliged to wait till the companies were ready to start, and surely if we had been natural or unnatural curiosities we could not have been commented on or stared at any more by the people surrounding us. 'Mormons, men, women and children, and worse, a lot of young girls, bound for Salt Lake and going to pull 'hand carts!' Shocking!'

" Yet, for the potent reason that no other way seemed open, and on the principle of ' descending below all things, ' I made up my mind to pull a hand cart. ' All the way to Zion,' a foot journey from Iowa to Utah, and pull our luggage, think of it! Anonymous letters, and warnings from sympathizing outsiders were mysteriously conveyed to us, setting forth the hardships and impossibilities of such a journey, and offering us inducements to stay. Many who started out with us backed out in a few days; my sister broke down and was unable to walk and I remember asking myself (footsore and weary with the first week of walking and working) if it was possible for me, faith or no faith, to walk twelve hundred miles further. The flesh certainly was weak but the spirit was willing, I set down my foot that I would try, and by the blessing of God I pulled a hand cart a thousand miles and never rode one step. Some thrilling scenes I could relate incident to that journey, but must forbear for want of space. Suffice it to say that after a long and wearisome journey, being entirely out of provisions, we halted for want of strength to proceed, and never should I have beheld (with mortal eyes) 'the city of the Saints' had not the compassionate people of Utah sent out a number of brave-hearted brethren with food and clothing to our relief. May they all be everlastingly blessed.

" In the month of June, 1857, firmly believing in the principle of plural marriage I entered into it. The result of this marriage was one child only, for a little more than three years after said marriage, my husband went on a mission to England, and after I had worked for upwards of four years to maintain myself and little one, my husband himself sent me word that he never intended to set foot in Utah again. And here I must be allowed to say in behalf of myself and other true women who have endured such separations, and to whom, perhaps, it is counted as nothing, no one can realize what such an ordeal is, unless they have passed through it. All that I had hitherto suffered seemed like child's play compared to being deserted by the one in whom I had chosen to place the utmost confidence, who himself had fixed an impassable gulf between us by ignoring the very principles by which he had obtained me, leaving myself and my little one (for all he knew) to sorrow and destitution. Harder still, was it for me to believe that this abandonment had been deliberately planned. I could not accept the fact till President Young, (speaking to me of my husband), emphatically said, ' Don't you know he asked for his mission? If he hadn't I wouldn't have sent him till the day of his death!' That was enough for me, I comprehended all that it meant, and independent of Brigham Young's word I was forced to believe it.

" I had striven hard to keep out of debt,—determined to do my part as a missionary's wife, that when my husband came back he might not be hampered on my account. Nevertheless 'hard times' stared me in the face, and I was almost overwhelmed by circumstances beyond my control. During the winter season of 1863-4, (owing to the war and many circumstances combined) provisions and other necessaries commanded almost fabulous prices, and I could not see how I should ever be able to keep 'the wolf from the door.' To add to my trouble, the house I occupied (and to which I had been led to believe I had some claim,) was sold over my head and thus I had the prospect of being homeless, at a time when rents were going up double and treble. One night when I was so weary with overwork and anxiety, pondering what to do, these words impressed me as if audibly spoken, TRUST IN GOD AND THYSELF. Instantly I arose and composed the following lines :

> A priceless boon! is a friend indeed
>   Greet him as such when his face you see;
> But those who fail thee in time of need—
>   Shun them, as false friends should shunned be.
> They proffer this, and they promise that,
>   But promise, alas, is a doubtful elf.

So would'st thou weather the storms of life—
  Trust thou in God! and thyself.

Keep a brave heart, though the waves roll high,
  Let thine aim be true as the magnet's steel ;
Look unto God! with a steadfast eye,
  And trust Him always, in woe or weal.
Man may deceive, but God! is true;
  Mortals may pander to love of pelf,
Like "Angel's visits" firm friends are few,
  Trust thou in God! and thyself,

Should friends, nor fortune, nor home be thine—
  Cringe not for this, nor beg for that ;
The earnest seekers will surely find
  Something to thoroughly labor at.
'Tis a cheering maxim to keep in view—
  That diligence leads to plenty's shelf;
And whatsoever thy hands pursue—
  Trust thou in God! and thyself.

What! though thy flesh and thy strength should fail?
  Surely 'were better to wear than rust ;
Than never to try, 'twere better to die,
  In striving bravely to fill our trust,
But fear not thou, for God! is good—
  He is the giver of strength and wealth .
When faithless feelings or friends intrude—
  Trust thou in God! and thyself.

" Immediately after this my way opened up before me,
almost within the week I secured another home, which if not
very commodious had for me the satisfying charm of being
my own.

" On May 7, 1864, I again entered into plural marriage, and
was sealed by Heber C. Kimball to Joseph Woodmansee, to
whom I have borne four sons and four daughters. Two of
these died in infancy, leaving me a family of seven, including
my first born.

" Nearly twenty years have rolled by since my second marriage, during which time I have seen many changes of fortune
which I cannot now relate, but I will say this much of my
children's father. Misfortunes that have befallen him have
never affected his faith, he has proven his allegiance to the

principles and priesthood of God at considerable sacrifice to himself and family, enduring reverses uncomplainingly.

"Of my children I need say but little, but I fervently hope that each and all of them may seek and obtain for themselves a knowledge of the truth, (called Mormonism) for I know it can make them wise unto salvation, and may they be willing if needs be to endure reproach and privation for principle's sake. I doubt not that all my troubles have been for my good, and to-day I am more than thankful for my standing in the Church of Jesus Christ of Latter-Day Saints."

> And wherefore should I cease to sing
>   Of Zion and the Latter Day?
> I could not find a nobler theme,
>   Nor choose a lovlier, loftier lay.
> Too insignificant is my praise—
>   Too feeble is my lyre and tongue,
> For of these longed for, Latter Days
>   Have royal bards and prophets sung.
>
> Ne'er shall our hearts ungrateful be;
>   Ne'er shall our songs be void of praise,
> For God has suffered us to see
>   "The Zion" of the Latter Days.
> Though all the world in scorn deride—
>   Our numbers shall not cease to flow;
> Our soul's sincerest, purest love
>   Thrills unto Zion's weal or woe.
>
> When she is sad, then I am sad;
>   When she is bound I am not free;
> When she is glad then I am glad
>   And all things prosper well with me.
> I love to see her power extend,
>   Her influence and her reign increase—
> Then wonder not, "for Zion's sake—
>   Will I not hold my peace."

"I desire to live to make up for past short-comings by future diligence, that I may help (in my humble way) to build up 'the kingdom whose dominion, power and greatness shall be given to the Saints of the most High! who shall possess it forever and ever.'"

12

The faith of the Saints shall astonish the world
And puzzle the wise to explain it;
Hosannah! hosannah! Truth's flag is unfurled,
And the Lord God Omnipotent reigneth.

HANNAH T. KING,

"The University town of Cambridge, England, I am proud to say, is the place of my nativity. I was reared among its classic shades and bowers. For the last thirty years America has been my adopted country, and I love her with a loyal and devoted appreciation, but the home and the haunts of childhood and youth leave on every mind indelible impressions and when brought to a focus upon the past as at the present moment, 'The distant spires and antique towers' rise up before me in all their vividness by the power of that most wonderful faculty, MEMORY.

"I was born and reared in the High Church of England, and nothing but the high Church of Jesus Christ of Latter-Day Saints could have caused me to secede from its high tenets and truly liberal principles; it stands second to none of the churches of the world.

"Any son or daughter might have been proud of such parents as mine, they were fine in person, highly moral, and intellectual, were descended from a highly born family, and were honored and respected by all who knew them; they reared their children with great care and watchfulness, giving them such an education as would fit them for all good society of whatever grade. Blessed be their memory!

"I was married at the early age of seventeen, but in my mind and character I was older than many girls at twenty. I have lived long enough to authorize the woman to sit in judgment on the girl.

"I had a sweet, happy home, for I had the faculty to make it so; I had ten beautiful children but death robbed me of several. We gave the surviving ones a liberal education with accomplishments; as they grew up they repaid us in being all we desired. From a child I had been accustomed to write much—keeping a journal and a book for choice extracts, etc. My father was unavoidably much away from home on business, but he enjoined me to write frequently to him, and to do *his* bidding was my delight, for he was my *beau ideal* of all that was good. Since at nine or ten I became a letter writer, and the thousands I have written in my long life would form a towering paper pillar. After some years of my married life I became a writer for the local papers and also wrote two books, one for my girls and the other for the boys, ' The Toilet ' and the ' Three Eras,' dedicating them to each. These books were patronized by the aristocracy of England. I also wrote considerable poetry all my life.

" In 1849, ' a change came o'er the spirit of my dream. ' I had a young woman who had worked for me eleven years as dressmaker, she was highly respectable, conscientious and good. In September, 1849, she was in the house at work, and on the evening of the 4th, when work was laid aside, she told me she wished to speak to me privately, as she had something she wished to communicate to me. I at once gave her the audience she requested and she then laid before me the organization of the Church of Jesus Christ of Latter-day Saints, with the first principles of the same. Of course I was startled! But the spirit of God witnessed to my spirit that she spoke *truth!* I compared all she told me by the Bible which had ever been my standard of truth—it *endorsed* all she said! I studied, I prayed,—she gave me to read 'Spencer's Letters'— they made me a willing convert. I read many other prominent works with which my teacher furnished me. Fifteen months passed, and yet I had not attended the Latter-Day Saint Meetings, or seen a single member but this young woman, yet even at that time I was a confirmed Latter-Day Saint. I then was introduced to an elder from America, and after his first sermon I was baptized by him in the classic waters of the Camm, my native river.

" Soon I began to see the antagonisms I had to meet. I, a

member of the Church of England. My grandfather a rector
in the same, my father and my mother, my family and friends!
All had to be met, could I bring the gray hairs of my parents
in sorrow to the grave? Could I reduce my family to compar-
ative poverty and reverses of every kind? Could I so lay my
all upon the altar of my God? Could I like Abraham of old,
arise and go to a far country—even the wilds of America? It
would take more than I have space to elaborate this subject—
suffice, strength was given me—I passed under 'the car of
Juggernaut,' which is no *overstrained* flower of language but a
veritable simile. Suffice, the votary lived! and I came out
convinced, determined, and the calm, as it were, of a summer
morning was upon me! A conviction had been given me that
it was indeed the work of the last days, when all dispensations
should be gathered in one, when that people I had all my life
prayed for in the Church of England should be ' prepared for
the second coming of the Savior,' were indeed organized upon
the earth by the voice of God Himself and His Son, Jesus
Christ, appearing to a youth, even Joseph Smith, and appoint-
ing him as the prophet of the last dispensation, under the
immediate direction of the Lord Jesus Himself. The Church
was organized with six members, on the 6th of April, 1830.

" Of this Church I became a member by the requisite act of
baptism by immersion, under the hands of the American missionary. From that time I had the spirit of 'gathering,' and
in June, 1853, I left my home and many that were dear to me,
my own immediate family accompanying me—and as I stood
on the deck of the *Golconda* I said, 'My native land, good
night.' Ox teams conveyed us over the prairies, and on the
19th of September, 1853, we entered Salt Lake City. Here
we built a home which has been my sanctuary. I *know* God
was with me, and my loved ones also were with me. The
union of my family was remarkable, that, and the Spirit of
God enabled us to ' remove mountains. '

"In a brief sketch like this it is impossible to give even
the outline, but could I place in a book, first our *antecedents,*
and then the marvelous events of those three years, the laying

aside our Lares and Penates, surely the skeptic would agree that there was a power with us that the world knows nothing of! for even though we *knew* we were the agents it was 'marvelous in our eyes.' Perhaps I have filled the brief space allotted me for the purpose for which I was called upon to write, surely my few words will be a testimony that I rejoice I am a Latter-Day Saint. I have passed through many reverses and tribulations, but in my darkest hours the Gospel has been a light upon my path and a lamp for my feet, and I realize day by day the smile and approbation of God upon me.

" It has been my delight to write for the Saints since I have lived in Salt Lake City, and my reward has been their love and rich appreciation of my writings. I have been a constant writer for the *Woman's Exponent*, a paper got up and entirely carried on by the women of our people. President Young desired me to write for it and I have done so with pleasure to the best of my ability, both in prose and in verse.

" For two years I had a school in my own house, and it promised to be a success, but my health failed, and to my sorrow I had to relinquish it. I was appointed to preside over the Young Ladies Mutual Improvement Association of the Seventeenth Ward, which position I held for one year, but resigned from feeble health. I was then appointed First Counselor to Marinda Hyde, President of the Relief Society of the Seventeenth Ward, which office I still have the honor to hold. My desire has ever been to be useful 'in my day and generation,' especially in the work of the last days, for in that I have joy and ample satisfaction.

"The history of the people of God as we read it in the Bible, repeats itself in a remarkable manner in the Church of Jesus Christ upon the earth to-day, and those who need a testimony of its truth, I advise them to compare and observe the workings of the self-same spirit of antagonism, and they will hardly need another. "

I select a portion of one of Mrs. King's poems; her prose and verse are alike, always lofty in character; her prose writings would form more than one valuable volume for the libraries of the Saints, or indeed those not of our faith. Historical and character sketches seem a peculiar gift with her. Among the many admirers of her poems the English Saints regard her with special fondness, for is she not their own? and they anticipate her contributions, as we look forward to flowers of spring, to summer's wealth of fruits, to autumn's harvest time.

REST.

" I've fought the battle all my life
Of outward foes and inward strife;
The strife which flesh and spirit feel
As keenly as the barbed steel;
For ah! my soul has longed to be
A perfect thing for God to see!
And feels impatient for the time
When I the heavenly heights shall climb,
The good, in all the ages past,
My eyes in love I've ever cast,
Would imitate, admire, and aim
Their glorious pinnacles to gain;
A pedestal to call my own,
One which my form might rest upon;
My spirit feet cannot yet stand
Upon the platform they command,
But well I know I have been blest,
And shall, in time, attain the rest;
And I have sometimes felt ere while
I moved 'neath God's effulgent smile
That shed around me warmth and peace,
And gave my captive mind release.
The earth and every living thing
Did tribute to my spirit bring;
And then my soul was born anew,
Begotten by the warmth and dew
Which God's own spirit cast around,
And placed my feet on holy ground.
All things seemed tinged with light of heaven,
My friends most loved, my foes forgiven!
The fountain in my heart, to me
Brought 'living water,' ecstacy!

*   *   *   *   *   *   *   *   *   *

A little Goshen was my home,
For joy and peace around it shone;

And labor's self became delight,
Making all healthy, strong and bright ;
And loving spirits gathered there
As angels—faithful, fond and fair.
Was I not blest? Yes, I was blest,
And truly 'twas a time of rest ;
Yes, rest from sorrow I had known ,
In youth, my sun but rarely shone,
But, oh! I-fought for joy and peace,
And God, in mercy, sent release.
And blest me with so bright a time
That's rarely known in earthly clime !
And grateful did my soul arise
To Him who gave this paradise.
But, oh ! this picture! its reverse!
A mighty contrast did disperse;
The light and warmth would be withdrawn
And I left freezing and forlorn;
The heavens seemed brass above my head,
The earth looked dark as molten lead ;
My God was hid beneath a cloud
And I, like corse within its shrond!
Alone, forsaken, desolate thing
Hoarding my sorrows like a sting
That probed and barbed my stranded soul,
And well-nigh crushed all self-control ;
The loved and loving were away,
And I to foes was left a prey ;
It seemed all blessings were withdrawn,
And I left stranded and forlorn,
To see if I would faithful stand
And still hold on to virtue's hand.
Yes, many such ordeal I've passed,
And know I have not seen the last.
Oh ! Father ! take my shrinking soul
Beneath Thy love and sweet control ;
Thy feeble, trembling child, oh spare!
Lay on no more than I can bear.
May I endure unto the end,
Whatever trials may portend ;
But Thou alone must bear me up,
Or I shall fail to drain the cup."

AUGUSTA JOYCE CROCHERON.

"In the original design of the picture Representative Women of Deseret, I did not include myself, but by the request of those whose wishes I have always endeavored to fulfill, now do so, although there are several to whom I would prefer giving place.

"I was born in Boston, Massachusetts, October 9, 1844. My father was John Joyce, from St. John, New Brunswick— his parents were both from England. I have heard my mother say that my uncle, Oliver Joyce, planted the English flag on the Chinese wall at the time of the war (about 1840) between those countries. I do not know whether he was an officer, color bearer or ordinary private.

"My mother, Caroline A. Joyce, was the eldest daughter of John Perkins, a sea captain, and his wife, Caroline Harriman. The Perkins and Harriman families were among the early Puritan emigrants, the property they first built upon still being in the possession of their descendants. I have heard my mother speak of the oak stairs and floors being so worn with age that they bent beneath the tread even when she was a child. My mother's mother was the daughter of Elder John Harriman, well known in New Hampshire as the occasional traveling companion of Lorenzo Dow, but more particularly as the founder of a sect called the 'New Light Christian Baptists.' He was the son of John Harriman and the daughter of a Penobscot chief who was friendly to the white people, and permitted his only daughter to receive Christian baptism, and she was afterwards married to him publicly in church. This union afforded peace and security to the settlers and gave them the alliance if needed, of a powerful tribe. The son of this marriage received an education and married. A few

13

weeks after, and at the age of twenty-one, he 'received a visit from a personage who gave him a new doctrine to preach to the children of men.' He awoke his wife, Ruth, told her the vision and she believed him. In the morning he began to arrange his worldly affairs so as not to interfere with his call and began to preach, accompanied by his young wife, who rose when he had done speaking and bore her testimony to what he had said. He traveled a certain circuit, holding two and three days' meetings wherever he stopped, building up quite a large church in his locality. He preached seventy-one years and died at the age of ninety-two. He never cut his hair from the time of his call to the ministry, and sometimes wore it braided in a queue, sometimes flowing in waves upon his shoulders, as in his portrait. His wife, Ruth, lived beyond her one hundredth birthday. His son, John, became a minister, but his daughter (my grandmother) was more worldly minded. Once when he entered the room she was standing before a mirror surveying her appearance, being attired for some special occasion. He quietly stepped up to her and with a pair of scissors cut off the long black ringlets that fell like a mantle upon her bare shoulders, saying; 'These come between you and your God.' This did not, however, quench the worldly spirit within her, for she at the age of sixteen eloped with and was married to John Perkins, a young sea captain, a God-fearing man but not a church member then or ever afterwards in this life. She was very industrious, however, and had at that age spun all her bed and table linen, etc. She became quite a politician and used to write articles of that character, and the young men of the town used to gather round her hearth and ask her opinion on political matters. She also composed for them campaign songs, both words and music. My mother has told me the only dancing she ever saw in her childhood was when her mother, inspired by the patriotic songs she would be singing, would dance to and fro at her spinning, instead of stepping—improvising step and figure. She had eight sons that she said she was 'raising for her country.' Sure enough two of them went to the war (twenty years ago) and laid down their lives; Warren and Andrew Jackson, (so named because he was born on the day of President Jackson's second inauguration.) Grandma was an Andrew Jackson Democrat, he was her very *beau ideal* of a man. Charles served two terms and returned safe. Lawrence, my patriot grandmother's youngest boy, enlisted at seventeen and was sent back; ' Too young,' they told him, but he waited one year and went again and this time they took him, and he too was spared to return home.

"Thaddeus sailed to Labrador through many years, and John to the West Indies. Her eldest daughter was my mother. When my mother heard and received the Gospel in Boston, she hastened home to bear the good tidings and obtain their permission for her baptism. She found them bitterly opposed to this, her father reticent, her mother reproachful. Just at this time Elder John Harriman arrived to hold a three days' meeting. Preparations had been made for his coming, and on his arrival my grandmother received him in her best parlor and after the usual salutations were over, unfolded to him the story of my mother's conversion, that she had gone insane and wanted to join the Mormons. He asked, ' Where is Caroline?' adding, reflectively, 'if the Lord has any more light for the children of men, I for one am willing to receive it. ' His grandchild, overhearing this, was filled with joy. Her mother came out and told her to put on her bonnet and shawl. Not knowing what was wanted of her to perform she obeyed, and by the time she was ready, found her brother, John, waiting with a horse and sleigh, and seating herself therein was rapidly whirled away to some relatives several miles distant, to remain there until sent for. Said she, ' I never saw my grandfather again.' This was a specimen of my grandma's executive ability; no circumlocution about her.

"I will give her own account of her receiving the Gospel, from a portion of her manuscripts :

" 'In the year 1842, I was living in the city of Boston, State of Massachusetts. One day I heard that a strange sect were

preaching in Boylston Hall, they professed to believe in the
same Gospel as taught by Jesus Christ and the ancient Apostles.
I went to hear them. As we entered the hall they were singing
a new song—the words were:

> 'The Spirit of God like a fire is burning,
> The Latter Day Glory begins to come forth,
> The visions and blessings of old are returning,
> The angels are coming to visit the earth.' &c.

"After the song a young man* arose and taking for his text
these words—'And in the last days it shall come to pass that
the Lord's House shall be established in the tops of the
mountains and all nations shall flow unto it,' said the time for
the fulfillment of this prophecy was near at hand, an angel
had appeared unto a man named Joseph Smith, having the
keys of the Everlasting Gospel to be preached to this generation,
that those who obeyed it would gather out from the wicked,
and prepare themselves for the coming of the Son of Man.
He spoke of the great work already commenced in these the
last days, and while I listened, his words were like unto a
song heard in my far off childhood, once forgotten but now
returning afresh to my memory, and I cried for very joy. I
went home to tell my father the good news, but my words
returned to my own heart, for both my parents thought me
insane, and talked to each other sadly of my condition and
what to do with me. My heart was filled with sorrow and
disappointment. I asked for the privilege of being baptized
but was answered with these words by my father: 'You
must leave home if you join those Mormons.' I went away
and was baptized for the remission of my sins, but still with
regret and an uncertainty as to the *right* to disobey my
parents. Soon after, my father left the city, and my mother
came and took me with her, to care for me, as she was fearful
I would be 'ruined by those deceivers.' One night I had been
to meeting where the Spirit of God seemed to fill the house,
and returned home thankful to my Heavenly Father that I

---

*Elder Erastus Snow. He afterward married her to her husband,
and blessed her children's children.

ever heard the Gospel. I laid down to rest beside my mother who commenced upbraiding me, and instantly I was filled with remorse that I was the cause of her unhappiness. I did not know what to say, and was hesitating, when, just over my head, a *voice*, not a whisper, but still and low, said these words: 'If you will leave father and mother, you shall have Eternal Life,' I asked, 'Mother, did you hear that?' She answered, '*You are bewitched!*' I knew then *she* had not heard the voice, but my mind was at rest and I went to sleep. I have heard the same voice since, not in dreams, but in daylight, when in trouble and uncertain which way to go; and I *know God lives* and guides this people called 'Mormons,' I know also the gifts and blessings are in the Church of Jesus Christ of Latter-Day Saints, and that same faith once delivered to the Saints is also ours, if we *live* for it.

" ' In the month of February, 1845, I left home, my native land and all the friends of my youthful days, and sailed in the ship, *Brooklyn*, for California. Before starting I visited my parents, then living in New Hampshire. I told them of my determination to follow God's people, who had already been notified to leave the United States, that our destination was the Pacific Coast, and we should take materials to plant a colony.

" ' When the hour came for parting, my father could not speak. My mother asked, ' When shall we see you again, my child?' I answered, ' *When there is a railroad across the continent.*' God grant that prophecy may be fulfilled and her life be spared to see it. I *knew* it would be there, even the ' highway cast up that the eagle's eye had never seen, nor the lion's foot had ever trod.'

"I turned my back on all once dear, for the memory of that voice was in my ears,—'If you will leave father and mother, you shall have eternal life,' and selling my household treasures, wrapped my child in my cloak (for the weather was bitter cold) and started on my long journey around the Horn.

" 'Of all the unpleasant memories, not one half so bitter as that dreary six months' voyage in an emigrant ship. We were so closely crowded that the heat of the Tropics was terrible, but 'mid all our trials the object of our journey was never forgotten. The living faith was there and was often manifested. I remember well one dreadful storm during which we had to be hatched below, as the waves broke over the ship, and filled our staterooms.

"'While the elements were raging above, and we below were being tossed about like feathers, the good old captain came down among us wearing a solemn countenance. We tried to gather around him; he said to us: ' My friends, there is a time in a man's life when it is fitting to prepare to die, and that time has come to us; I have done all I *can do*, but, unless God interposes we *must go down*.' A good sister answered, ' Captain, we *were sent to California and we shall go there*.' He went up stairs, saying, ' *These people have a faith I have not.* ' And so it proved. We outrode the storm, we endured another off Cape Horn; we stopped and buried one of our dear sisters, a mother of seven children, (Mrs. Goodwin) at Juan Fernandez, and at last reached our new home, the last day of July, 1846, to find a country at war with our own government, a country barren and dreary, so unlike the California of to-day, but we trusted in God and he heard our prayers; and when I soaked the mouldy ship bread purchased from the whaleships lying in the harbor, (returned from a four years' cruise) and fried it in the tallow taken from the rawhides lying on the beach, God made it sweet to me and to my child, for on this food I weaned her. I used to think of Hagar and her babe, and of the God who watched over them, and again I remembered the voice and the words it spoke unto me—and took courage.

"'From that day to this, I can bear my testimony to all the world that I have known, and still know, this is the work of God and will exalt us if we seek to know His will, and knowing it, do it. '

"My mother's testimony, written at my request, was the last work performed by her hand. After finishing, she accompanied a caller to the gate, the chill night air penetrated her frame and morning found her sick with pneumonia. From that bed she was borne seven days later, from the earthly gaze of children and friends forever. They called it death, but to her it was the reward promised, and recorded by her own hand—'Eternal Life.'

"My mother had kept a daily journal on the ship, *Brooklyn*, also the first five or six years in San Francisco, calling it 'The Early Annals of California.' This I considered invaluable from the reliability and the fullness of its historic matter and data, and after her demise I searched for it but it was gone. This I thought strange indeed, for she had assured me of its preservation about eighteen months before her last illness. I have heard her relate many incidents of those times. Once when nearly famished, (hostilities not yet being concluded between Mexico and the United States,) two men ventured outside the town to lasso one of the cattle browsing so near them, but were themselves caught by cruel Mexicans in ambush, and killed and quartered, their bodies left lying on the sand in view of the wretched inhabitants. At another time a Mexican was intercepted and searched. In one boot was found an order from General Castro, to attack by night and kill everything above four years old that could speak English. The messenger was buried in the sand. After awhile the native women became curious, and some of them ventured past the guard after dark, and being touched with compassion, returned in the same cautious manner, with bottles of *leche* (milk) slung around their waists under their flounced dress skirts, and *tortillas* (flour and water cakes) concealed beneath their *revosas* (mantles,) for the women and children Soon after the landing the brethren strayed around, glad to be on land and looking to see what they could find. 'Any fruit?' asked one of a returning comrade. 'Yes,' said he, 'grape, lots of 'em.' There was a rush off in that direction and a fruitless search. Being sharply questioned, he pulled a handful of grape shot out of his pocket, which he had picked up from the scene of a recent engagement. The same day a gentleman passenger, traveling for pleasure, brought a bouquet of wild flowers to

me, saying: 'Little lady, I herewith present you the first bouquet ever offered by a white man to a white woman in Yerba
Buena.' Yerba Buena was the original name of San Francisco,
and means 'good herb'—from a kind of pennyroyal growing
wild there at that time. My mother kept the flowers many
years and told me the story over their odorless ashes. My father
and mother with many of the Saints, (sixteen families) moved
from the ship into the 'old adobie,' partitioned off with quilts.
Soon after he rented a house, but the largest room was required of him as a hospital for the wounded soldiers; the next
largest for a printing office. The press was an old Spanish
press, and there being no *W* in that alphabet, they used to
turn the *M* upside down. My mother used to help decipher
the dispatches, many of them being written on the battlefield
with a burnt stick or coal.

" Her first Christmas dinner in San Francisco consisted of
a quart of beans and a pound of salt pork, which the hospital
steward brought to her; he told her he would be flogged if it
became known. In after days he became her steward. One
day Dr. Poet, surgeon of the navy, brought my mother a slice
of ham, a drawing of tea and a lump of butter about the size
of a walnut. Dr. Poet had told my father where he could pur-
chase half a barrel of flour. After baking some flour and water
cakes between two tin plates in the ashes, my mother brought
her dear friend, Mrs. Robbins, (now in this city,) to share the
repast. Said Mrs. Robbins: 'Mrs. Joyce, isn't this like
Boston?' This was just after living for six months on mouldy
shipbread. I have heard her say that often she was so hungry
she would willingly have walked ten miles to obtain a slice of
bread. Soon after this my mother helped to take care of the
' Donner Party, ' who were found partly frozen and so famished
that they were eating their dead companions. The girl she
tended, told her that they grew to like it, and she had helped
eat her brother. The true stories they told are too dreadful to
repeat, particularly as some of them are still living. The
Mormon Battallion came; peace was declared, the gold mines
were discovered, and the circumstances of the Saints were

changed from isolation and famine to wealth and grandeur. My father became very wealthy, but prosperity caused his apostacy. My grandfather, and uncle, John Perkins, both sea captains, came to see my mother. I well remember sitting on grandpa's knee and learning my alphabet from the large family Bible spread before him, he being my teacher. I often recall also the long evenings when Uncle John held me on his knee and sang the strange, pathetic, old-fashioned sea songs of which he knew so many and sang them so sweetly; I used to nestle closer to him, half frightened, and at last fall asleep. I remember one was, ' 'Twas down in the lowlands a poor boy did wander, ' and I have never heard it since.

"In Boston my mother was called 'The Mormon nightingale.' Strangers indifferent to the Gospel would say, ' Let us go to Boylston Hall and hear the singing.' A gentleman of fortune offered to take her to Italy and educate her in singing, at the same time that Adelaide Philips (his protege) went, but her destiny was upon another stage, to sing the hymns of the newly-restored Gospel; and many have thought that she sang them as one inspired. Her rendering of Wm. Clayton's hymn, 'The Resurrection Day,' will be remembered by all who ever heard it. She purchased the first melodeon brought to San Francisco, (by a Mr. Washington Holbrook,) thereby causing a sensation among the wives of the ministers of five denominations, who each wanted it for their church. She went, during the ravages of the cholera, in San Francisco, and gathered together sixty orphan children, providing for them until a building spot, material and means were collected by subscription; and was one of the Board of managers of the Protestant Orphan Asylum thus originated and founded. I remember going with her and hearing the children sing, ' The Watcher,' a song of poverty and death. At the expiration of one year some of the ladies objected to having a Mormon officer among them, ' not considering Mormonism a religion at all,' although quite willing to accept the continuance of her contributions. She however found a larger and more congenial field of labor; brethren going on their missions, their families left behind in

14

Utah, received her prompt remembrance. Also seeds, trees, &c., she sent to Utah spring and fall, through more than twenty years. My only sister was born in San Francisco, August, 1847, and died in St. George, Mrs. Helen F. Judd, one of the truest Saints I ever knew. In San Francisco Parley P. Pratt was a guest at my mother's house. She had loaned the Book of Mormon to a gentleman belonging to the Custom House; Colonel Alden A. M. Jackson. He had been in the Mexican War, at the battle of Buena Vista, and was with General Scott and Zachary Taylor through that campaign. He had two horses killed under him and received injuries that lasted throughout his life. When he returned the book he said he had read it day and night until finished, and wished to know where he could find a minister of the Mormon Church. She invited him to come that evening and meet the Apostle, author and poet, Parley P. Pratt. The gentlemen became so interested in their theme that my mother left the room without disturbing them, and giving a servant instructions to attend to Mr. Pratt's room, etc., retired. Descending the stairs next morning she heard Brother Pratt conversing, the lamp still burning. 'Good morning, géntlemen,' said she; Brother Pratt looked up—'Is it morning?' Colonel Jackson walked to the window—'Yes,' said he, 'another day has dawned, and another day has dawned for me—a beautiful one.' Brother Pratt looked out upon the garden and said significantly, 'It only needs water to complete the picture.' Colonel Jackson replied, 'I understand you, I am ready.' Turning to my mother Brother Pratt asked, 'Sister Joyce, have you renewed your covenants? A number are going to the North Beach to-morrow, will you go?' and she answered thoughtfully, 'Ten years ago last night I was baptized in the Atlantic at midnight; to-morrow I will be baptized in the Pacific.'

"My own parents had been separated since my father's apostacy. A few months after her baptism she moved to San Bernardino and there began building a beautiful home. Colonel Jackson, on his way to Utah was delayed, waiting for a train to cross the deserts, and my mother being his only acquaintance, he often sought her society, and at last determined to win her if possible, and some three years after their first acquaintance they were married. Never was a kinder father than he. Years added to years drew us all nearer to each other.

" In 1856, at the time of the Utah War, an armed mob of twenty-two men visited the four remaining Mormon families in San Bernardino, and calling father out from breakfast, ordered him to leave town with his family by nine o'clock. He replied he would not do it, prefacing and concluding the reply in language more forcible than elegant. They planted an old cannon on the public square, fired it off, rode around and threatened a great deal. Father's law office fronted the square; he went as usual to it, and in the afternoon they made a bonfire outside and coming in to him told him they intended to burn him alive. He continued writing, only telling them if they disturbed his papers he would send daylight through them. They left. When we were all ready to start for Utah, enemies obtained a writ from the court prohibiting my sister and I from leaving the State before we were of age. We were among enemies and powerless. My mother said, ' If we can't go, our property shall,' and with father's consent divided goods, provisions, arms and ammunition with the poor who could go. In 1864, my mother, sister and I came to Utah on a visit, returned here in 1867. In 1868 I was appointed Secretary of the Relief Society in St. George. In 1869 our parents brought us 'to the city' to receive our endowments, for which our joy and gratitude was beyond expression. I remained here, they returned to St. George where my sister married. In 1870 I became the second wife of George W. Crocheron. I believed I should better please my Heavenly Father by so doing than by marrying otherwise. Any woman, no matter how selfish, can be a first and only wife, but it takes a great deal more christian philosophy and fortitude and self-discipline to be a wife in this order of marriage; and I believe those who choose the latter when both are equally possible, and do right therein, casting out all selfishness, judging self and not another, have attained a height, a mental power, a spiritual plane above those who have not. To do this is to overcome that which has its roots in selfishness, and it can be done if each will do what is right. In November, 1870, I was appointed Secretary of the Young Ladies Mutual Improvement Association of the Ninth Ward, which position I filled till home duties compelled my resignation. At times during thirteen years I have reported, in the sisters' meetings, chiefly those of the Fourteenth Ward. In 1876 our father died, and in five weeks after our mother followed him. Their graves are side by side in the valley of St. George, as beautiful as we could make them.

"In 1878 I was appointed, and later, set apart and blessed to labor as Secretary of the Young Ladies Mutual Improvement Association for the Salt Lake Stake of Zion, which position I strive to honorably fill. In 1880, by the advice and aid of my friends I published a volume of poems, 'Wild Flowers of Deseret,' which was kindly received, the entire edition being sold within two years. The design of the picture Representative Women of Deseret, appeared to me one night as I rose from family prayers. I had not thought of it before. This book of biographical sketches to accompany it was an after thought. Many suppose that Mormon women are not encouraged in their abilities, are perhaps repressed. This has not been so in my case, or in my observations of others. Both encouragement and help have been given me by friends, by those in authority, and my husband has also encouraged and assisted me in every way in his power.

"I am the mother of three boys and two girls, born in the New and Everlasting Covenant, and consecrated to my Creator before I ever held them in my arms or pressed a mother's kiss upon their little faces. Myself and all that are mine to give are dedicated to the service of God, praying that He will help us to be worthy of His acceptance."

HELEN MAR WHITNEY,

Helen Mar Whitney was the third child of Heber Chase Kimball and his wife, Vilate Murray, and was born in Mendon, Munro County, New York, August 22, 1828. Their ancestors were among the Pilgrims and her kindred prided themselves that they were descended from a noble stock. Though they cared little for nobility and rank, they were proud to know that their grandsires who would not submit to tyranny and oppression, helped to gain them independence, and that their descendants were noble, hard working, self-sacrificing and conscientious people, who believed in rising by their own merits. Many of her ancestors died fighting for the liberty which is denied to some of their children, by men who have usurped authority and become oppressors. She was five years old when her parents removed to Kirtland, Ohio. In the winter of 1837, she was baptized by Brigham Young, her father cutting the ice for that purpose.

She inherited a reverence for the Supreme Being and always received the best teachings from her parents. Her father's time was mostly spent in the ministry. On his return from a European mission, he heard Joseph teach the principle of celestial marriage, and was commanded by Joseph to take a certain lady for his second wife. He felt as though he could not obey this and live in it, and must be released from the command, and he expressed the same to Joseph, who went and inquired of the Lord, and receiving an answer, commanded him the third time before he obeyed. Her mother bore testimony that she also went to the Lord and plead with Him to show her the cause of her husband's trouble, which his haggard face and wretched days and nights betrayed and he dared not tell her. He told her to go to the Lord and she did so, and He answered their prayers. She saw a vision and the principle was revealed to her in all its glory. She saw the woman that he had taken, and she went to him and told him what the Lord had shown her. She said she never saw him so happy, and he cried for joy. She took the second wife to her bosom, and from that time an unkind word never passed between them. Helen knew nothing of the order till June, 1843, wher her father revealed it to her. She says of this: "Had I not known he loved me too tenderly to introduce anything that was not strictly pure and exalting in its tendencies, I could not have believed such a doctrine. I could have sooner believed that he would slay me, than teach me an impure principle. I heard the Prophet teach it more fully, and in the presence of my father and mother.

"On the 3rd of February, 1846, I was married to H. K. Whitney, eldest son of N. K. Whitney, by Brigham Young. We were the last couple sealed in the Temple at Nauvoo. We were among the exiles who crossed the river on the 16th of the same month, intending to go over to the Rocky Mountains that year. But when the government demanded the strength of our companies to fight for them, we had to seek a place to quarter for the winter. I was sick most of the time while there. Some of the journey we had to walk, and our food being poor and scant, the infant and the aged, all classes, were swept off by death—the latter by scurvy and sheer exhaustion. The next year my husband was one of those chosen to go as a pioneer, and he had to go though the day of trial was upon me.

"Our first born, a lovely girl baby, was buried there—we could not both live; but during those dark hours I had friends and the Lord was there. We had but few men, mostly aged and disabled, but to see the union of the sisters; the fasting and prayers for the preservation of our battallion and the pioneers; and for the destroyer to be stayed; the great and marvelous manifestations, even the power of the resurrection, experienced there—proved that they were encircled by a mighty power, and that 'the prayers of the righteous availeth much.' I will mention one circumstance to show the heavenly spirit that dwelt with us there, and also the power of the destroyer, which none who witnessed could misunderstand.

"We were struggling with the evil one who had laid his grasp upon the babes—one was my mother's, the other, Sarah Ann's, (one of my father's wives). We all felt that we must part with one, as one would no sooner get relief than the other would be worse, and after a time mother asked the Lord, if agreeable to His will, to take hers and spare the other, as she had other children, and Sarah Ann had but this one. But He chose to take the latter. Should not this teach us a lesson? and where could such love be found, only in the hearts of *Saints?*

"Many weeks I remained feeble, but I had received the promise that I should be healed, and one morning Sister Perris Young, on whom the spirit had rested all night, to come and administer to me; came and under her administration, with my mother, I was made whole.

"Those were trying days, when one meal was eaten we knew not where we were to get the next, but we neither wanted for food nor raiment. We had not heard from the pioneers since they left till they were returning, and the news was that they were short of teams and without breadstuff, and a long way from home. Our feelings can better be imagined than described, for we had little enough ourselves, but we lifted our hearts to God, and I can call it nothing less than miraculous, a supply was soon furnished and men and teams started to meet them. The next spring all were preparing to move, and as I was helping to put on my wagon cover I came near fainting and was prostrated on my bed from that time. I had a baby boy born on the 17th of August, but he was buried on the 22nd, my twentieth birthday. This was the worst part of our journey, the roads being rough and rocky. I mourned incessantly, and that with my intense bodily sufferings soon brought me to death's door, but it was shorn of its sting. I was cold, but oh, how peaceful, as I lay there painless and my breath passing so gently away; I felt as

though I was wafting on the air and happy in the thought of
meeting so soon with my babes where no more pain or sorrow
could come. I had talked with my husband and father who
were weeping as I took a parting kiss from all but my poor
mother, who was the last one called and had sunk upon her
knees before me. This distressed me, but I bade her not
mourn for she would not be long behind me. My words struck
father like a sudden thunderbolt, and he spoke with a mighty
voice and said—'Vilate, Helen *is not dying!*' but my breath
which by this time had nearly gone, stopped that very instant,
and I felt his faith and knew that he was holding me; and I
begged him to let me go as I thought it very cruel to keep me,
and believed it impossible for me to live and ever recover. The
destroyer was then stirred up in anger at being cheated out of
his victim and he seemed determined to wreak his vengeance
upon us all. No one but God and the angels to whom I owe
my life and all I have, could know the tenth part of what I
suffered. I never told anybody and I never could. A keener
taste of misery and woe, no mortal, I think, could endure.
For three months I lay a portion of the time like one dead,
they told me; but that did not last long. I was alive to my
spiritual condition and dead to the world. I tasted of the
punishment which is prepared for those who reject any of the
principles of this Gospel. Then I learned that plural marriage was a celestial principle, and saw the difference between
the power of God's priesthood and that of Satan's and the
necessity of obedience to those who hold the priesthood, and
the danger of rebelling against or speaking lightly of the
Lord's annointed.

"I had, in hours of temptation, when seeing the trials of my
mother, felt to rebel. I hated polygamy in my heart, I had
loved my baby more than my God, and mourned for it unrea-
sonably. All my sins and shortcomings were magnified before
my eyes till I believed I had sinned beyond redemption. Some
may call it the fruits of a diseased brain. There is nothing
without a cause, be that as it may, it was a keen reality to me.
During that season I lost my speech, forgot the names of

everybody and everything, and was living in another sphere, learning lessons that would serve me in future times to keep me in the narrow way. I was left a poor wreck of what I had been, but the Devil with all his cunning, little thought that he was fitting and preparing my heart to fulfill its destiny. My father said that Satan desired to clip my glory and was quite willing I should die happy; but when he was thwarted he tried in every possible way to destroy my tabernacle. President Young said that the mountains through which we passed were filled with the spirits of the Gadianton robbers spoken of in the Book of Mormon. The Lord gave father faith enough to hold me until I was capable of exercising it for myself. I was so weak that I was often discouraged in trying to pray, as the evil spirits caused me to feel that it was no use: but the night after the first Christmas in this valley, I had my last struggle and resolved that they should buffet me no longer. I fasted for one week, and every day I gained till I had won the victory and I was just as sensible of the presence of holy spirits around my bedside as I had been of the evil ones. It would take up too much room to relate my experience with the spirits, but New Year's eve, after spending one of the happiest days of my life I was moved upon to talk to my mother. I knew her heart was weighed down in sorrow and I was full of the holy Ghost. I talked as I never did before, I was too weak to talk with such a voice (of my own strength), beside, I never before spoke with such eloquence, and she knew that it was not myself. She was so affected that she sobbed till I ceased. I assured her that father loved her, but he had a work to do, she must rise above her feelings and seek for the Holy Comforter, and though it rent her heart she must uphold him, for he in taking other wives had done it only in obedience to a holy principle. Much more I said, and when I ceased, she wiped her eyes and told me to rest. I had not felt tired till she said this, but commenced then to feel myself sinking away. I silently prayed to be renewed, when my strength returned that instant.

"New Year's day father had set apart to fast and pray, and they prepared a feast at evening. I had prayed that I might

15

gain a sure testimony that day that I was acceptable to God, and my father, when he arose to speak, was so filled with His power, that he looked almost transfigured! He turned to me and spoke of my sufferings and the blessings I should receive because of the same. He prophesied of the great work that I should do, that I should live long and raise honorable sons and daughters that would rise up and call me blessed, and should be a comfort to my mother in her declining years, and many more things which I have fulfilled. Many who knew me then have looked at me and seen me working with my children around me, with perfect amazement and as one who had been dead and resurrected.

" I lost three babes before I kept any, (two boys and girl). My first to live was Vilate, she grew to womanhood and was taken. Orson F. was my next, who has been appointed Bishop of the Eighteenth Ward. I had four more daughters, then a son, my last a little girl who died at five years of age; being eleven in all. My parents have left me and my heart has been wrung to the utmost, yet I have said—*Thy will O God, be done.* Persons have sometimes wondered at my calmness and endurance, but I think they would not had they passed through the same experience.

" I have encouraged and sustained my husband in the celestial order of marriage because I knew it was right. At various times I have been healed by the washing and annointing, administered by the mothers in Israel. I am still spared to testify to the truth and Godliness of this work; and though my happiness once consisted in laboring for those I love, the Lord has seen fit to deprive me of bodily strength, and taught me to 'cast my bread upon the waters' and after many days my longing spirit was cheered with the knowledge that He had a work for me to do, and with Him, I know that all things are possible.

" Almost my first literary effort was inspired by the reading of the various opinions of men published in our dailies, upon woman's disabilities, etc.; and my continuing is due to the advice and urgent wishes of many of my sisters.

"On March 10, 1882, I was chosen by Sister M. I. Horne and nominated to act as her Counselor in the Relief Society of this stake of Zion in place of Sister S. M. Heywood (deceased) and God grant that I may come up to her standard and be able to labor faithfully with my sisters yet many years, in relieving and comforting the tried and afflicted, and enlightening the minds of those who are in darkness concerning the things of God and His people."

It is but appropriate and just to add to the brief sketch of Helen Mar Whitney's life, a brief record of her son, the eldest of her living children.

Orson F. Whitney was born in Salt Lake City, July 1, 1855. Was called on his first mission during the October Conference of 1876. Left home for Pennsylvania November 6th following. Remained in Pennsylvania about five months, laboring with Elder A. M. Musser, and visited Washington just prior to the inauguration of President Hayes. Early in the spring of 1877 went alone down to Ohio, where he remained about one year, preaching and baptizing, and visiting relatives in and around Kirtland, (his father's birthplace). Was released from his mission in the spring of 1878, and returned home early in April. Was appointed a home missionary immediately on his return, and also obtained a situation in the *Deseret News* office.

July 14th, was ordained a High Priest, (previously was a Seventy) and set apart to preside as bishop of the Eighteenth Ward, being the youngest bishop in the Salt Lake Stake of Zion, succeeding Bishop L. D. Young, resigned. August 10th of same year succeeded Elder John Nicholson as city editor of the *Deseret News*, he having been called to Europe on a mission. Before this he had labored as a collector and under-clerk in the business office of that establishment. During his sojourn in the States he had corresponded with the *Salt Lake Herald*, the *Woman's Exponent* and the *News*, to the latter by the direct invitation of President Brigham Young, who had noticed his writings to the other papers and urged him to cultivate his literary ability. Previously he had scarcely dared to hope he possessed any. He says of this; "I owe much to the kind encouragement of President Young for what little I have yet achieved in that direction."

December 18, 1879, was married to Zina B. Smoot, daughter of President A. O. and Mrs. Emily Smoot. In February, 1880, was elected to the City Council and held the office of a Councilor until called on his second mission, whither he went before his office term had expired. In July, 1880, was appointed by a committee having in charge the arrangement of a programme to celebrate the fiftieth anniversary of the Church (year of jubilee,) to write a poem for the occasion. The poem —"Jubilee of Zion," was read in the Tabernacle by Colonel David McKenzie, on the 24th of July, the Jubilee Celebration and the regular Pioneer Day Celebration being blended. Prior to this he had published a pamphlet containing two poems, "Land of Shinehah" and the "Women of the Everlasting Covenant," and had contributed various efforts in verse to our local papers, besides other articles in prose to the *Contributor* and *Herald*, at the same time laboring regularly upon the *News* as local editor. April, 1880 (antedating the above), the Home Dramatic Club was organized with O. F. Whitney as President.

October, 1880, the first child of Bishop Whitney, a son, was born. June 20, 1881, at a meeting of the General Committee on celebration of the 4th of July, Bishop Whitney was chosen Orator of the Day, and prepared the oration, the assassination of President Garfield on the 2nd of July put a stop to the celebration, and consequently to the carrying out of the programme. October Conference, 1881, was called on a mission to England and left October 24th; sailed from New York November 1st, and landed on the 10th. Appointed to the London Conference, labored there four months; then called to Liverpool to succeed Elder C. W. Stayner in the editorial department of the *Millennial Star*. Labored there nearly a year, then was released to travel in the ministry. Released to return home with the June company, 1883. Visited Scotland and France and sailed for home June 20th. Landed in New York Sunday, July 1st, the very day and date of his birth, twenty-eight years before. Reached home July 7, 1883, and has resumed his position as city editor of the *Deseret Evening News.*

LETTERS OF HEBER C. KIMBALL.

For the consideration of those unacquainted with him, who through misreport have been led to regard Heber C. Kimball as a man of stern rule and cold nature, I append two letters written by him to his beloved first wife, Vilate, (a name that is revered in our people's remembrance) showing in true light his own feelings upon the principle of plural marriage and vindicating and honoring him by this testimony from his own secret heart and lips, better than the words of another, no matter how faithful or true or ardent that friend might be. Thus will be shown to the world three generations of a family who are representatives of our people and faith; Heber, one whom God chose as one of the first to aid in founding and up-building His Church and Kingdom in the last dispensation; Helen, his cherished and heroic daughter, and Orson, her son, worthy representative of his mother and grandfather. The inspiration in Heber's life has not died out in theirs, the work has not slackened, the line of march is still onward and upward. The first copy bears date of

" October 23, 1842.

" *My Dear Vilate:*

"I am at Brother Evan Green's. We have held all our conferences, have had two meetings to-day, it being the Sabbath. Some have been added to the Church and prejudice is considerably laid. Monday we shall go to Jacksonville, then on to Springfield. I shall be home in two or three weeks if the Lord wills it so. Since I left you it has been a time of much reflection. I felt as though I was a poor weak creature in and of myself, and only on God can I rely for support. I have been looking back over my past life before I heard the

Gospel. It makes me shrink into nothing and to wish I had always been a righteous man from my youth, but we have an advocate with the Father, and I can look back since I came into the Church of Jesus Christ of Latter-Day Saints, with a degree of pleasure, but I can see if I had more knowledge I could have done better in many points. * * I feel as though I had rather die to-day than be left to transgress one of His laws, or to bring disgrace upon the cause which I have embraced, or a stain upon my character; and my prayer is day by day that God would take me to Himself rather than I should be left to sin against Him, or betray my dear brethren who have been true to me and to God the Eternal Father, and I feel to pray to Thee, O Lord, to help thy poor servant to be true to Thee all the days of my life, that I may never be left to sin against Thee or against Thy annointed, or any that love thee, that I may have wisdom and knowledge how to gain Thy favor at all times, for this is my desire, and that these blessings may rest upon my dear companion, and when we have done Thy work on this Thy footstool, that Thou wouldst receive us into that kingdom where Abraham, Isaac and Jacob and all the holy prophets have gone, that we may never be separated any more, and before I should be left to betray my brethren in any case, let Thy servant come unto Thee in Thy Kingdom and there have the love of my youth, and the little ones Thou has given me. * * Now, my dear Vilate, stand by me even unto death, and when you pray, pray that I may hold out to the end. * * My heart aches for you and sometimes I can hardly speak without weeping, and that before my brethren: for I have a broken heart and my head is a fountain of tears. My life in this world is short at the longest, and I do not desire to live one day only to do good and to make you happy and bring up our little children in the ways of the Lord, and my prayer is that they may be righteous from the least to the greatest. * * The world has lost its charms for me, and I want to seek for that rest which remains for the people of God. I never had a greater desire to be a man of God than at the present, that I may know my acceptance with Him. ''

"SPRINGFIELD, October 25th.

" *My Dear Companion:*

"I have just returned from the office where I found a letter from you, and I need not tell you that it was a sweet morsel to me. I could weep like a child if I could get away by myself, to think that I for one moment have been the means of causing you any sorrow; I know that you must have many bad feelings and I feel to pray for you all the time, I assure you that you have not been out of my mind many minutes at a time since I left you. My feelings are of that kind that it makes me sick at heart, so that I have no appetite to eat. My temptations are so severe it seems sometimes as though I should have to lay down and die, I feel as if I should sink beneath it. I go into the woods every chance I have, and pour out my soul before God that He would deliver me and bless you, my dear wife, and the first I would know I would be in tears, weeping like a child about you and the situation I am in; but what can I do but go ahead? My dear Vilate, do not let it cast you down, for the Lord is on our side; this I know from what I see and realize and I marvel at it many times. You are tried and tempted and I am sorry for you, for I know how to pity you. I can say that I never suffered more in all my life than since these things came to pass; and as 1 have said so say I again, I have felt as if I should sink and die. Oh my God! I ask Thee in the name of Jesus to bless my dear Vilate and comfort her heart and deliver her from temptation and sorrow, and open her eyes and let her see things as they are, for Father Thou knowest our sorrow; be pleased to look upon Thy poor servant and handmaid, and grant us the privilege of living the same length of time that one may not go before the other, for Thou knowest that we desire this with all our hearts. * * * And then, Father, when we have done with our career in this probation, in the one to come may we still be joined in one to remain so to all eternities, and whatever we have done to grieve Thee be pleased to blot it out, and let us be clean and pure before Thee at all times, that we may never be left to sin or betray anyone that believes on Thy name; save us from all this and let our seeds be righteous; incline their hearts to be pure and virtuous, and may this extend from generation to generation, let us have favor in Thy sight and before Thine angels that we may be watched over by them and have strength and grace to support us in the day of our temptation that we may not be overcome and fall.   Now my Father, these are the desires of our hearts, and wilt Thou grant them to us for Jesus' sake and to Thy name will we give all the glory forever and ever. "

ZINA Y. WILLIAMS.

DAUGHTER OF BRIGHAM YOUNG.

It would be strange indeed, if after the life and labors of Brigham Young, a work of this character should appear, lacking the name and record of his descendants. The sons of noble men have greater opportunities of adding lustre to their father's name by reason of the advantages which sons possess over daughters; yet among our people, women have their acknowledged province in which they may distinguish themselves, in which their position is not borrowed from the other sex, or an infringement upon them; and yet may adorn the memory of even Brigham Young. Such a daughter is Zina Y. Williams, the original of this sketch. Born in plural or celestial marriage, and with an understanding of this condition, as much as any young girl can possess, a wife in the same order of marriage.

Some have said, "Let us see the workings of this system, let us see how the next generation will receive it." The time has come when they can see, and learn that those who understand it best fear it least. The words of the daughter herself, it seems to me, should go farther in effect than mine could for her. Here is a true picture in the home life of the earliest advocates of that ancient principle, restored through Joseph Smith, the prophet. I have known Mrs. Williams beneath her father's roof and in her own married home, intimately, for eighteen years, and knew the union and love of the band of sisters.

"I was born April 3rd, 1850, in Salt Lake City. My mother, Zina H. Young, was made glad by my presence, her only

16

daughter. My father, President Brigham Young, made me
welcome; though he was the father of many others he was as
much pleased as many men are over their only girl. My
childhood was clouded with sickness, and one of my earliest
recollections is of my loving mother holding me in her arms,
singing a sweet song; with the moonlight streaming over me
and gazing out upon the full moon I sank to sleep, soothed
from suffering by her magic care. I was the pet of my two
brothers and of all my mother's friends. I knew nothing of
want or care till the year of famine, (1856) which gave me a
faint idea of what want was. (All through the Territory families
were on short rations.)

" My father's family lived in a world of their own, there being ten girls with not more than four years' difference in their
ages. Our father affectionately called us his 'big ten,' and
nowhere on the earth could be found a happier, merrier set of
children. We attended school and were instructed in music
and dancing on our own premises. Our mothers taught us to
respect each other's rights, as they always set the example by
treating one another according to the golden rule. A person
entering the room where we were assembled would be at a
loss to tell which were the own children of the sisters present.
We carried out the proverb—' Love thy neighbor as thyself, '
literally. When the memorable exodus of 1858 took place,
my mother was the first woman who left Salt Lake City. In
company with another of my father's wives, Lucy B., (as she
is called,) we started south. This was my first trip from home,
it seemed like a pleasure trip to me and it was a matter of
surprise that my dear mother and auntie were not as much
delighted with the change as we children were; but the sub-
sequent discomforts we were subjected to, and our lonely
hours spent away from our dearly loved sisters caused many a
heart pang and we began to realize something of the sacrifices
made by our people when our enemies came and invaded our
homes. My mother was the last of father's family to leave
Provo, after the return of the people to their former homes.
On our arrival, after a year's absence, father asked mother to

take charge of four of his little ones whose mother was dead. She consented, and this event entirely changed my after life; from being the pet and only child I now had to share with these motherless children. It was a trial in many ways, but my precious mother taught me to be unselfish and thank God for all His blessings and not complain, and I am thankful to say, following her advice without once alluding to the fact that my mother was not their own. Thus it proved to be the best lesson of my life, and a great blessing.

"My life flowed on in peaceful current, going to school, but going upon the stage when quite young greatly impaired my health. I married when eighteen. My husband, Thomas Williams, had been in my father's employ in his office, for several years; then in the Theatre, where I saw him frequently, but, as he was much older than I, it never occurred to me to fall in love with him. 'None knew him but to love him,' the bard wrote, which is true of my husband. I was his second wife, and here let me testify that in entering into the order of plural marriage, both my husband and myself did so from the purest and holiest motives. For six years I was his loving wife, bearing two sons, Sterling and Thomas Edgar. In July, 1873, my dear husband was called home. None but those who are called upon to pass through similar circumstances can know the sorrow and anguish it is to part from a loving, noble husband and father.

"My time now was given principally to my Church duties and to the support of my dear children. In all my trials my dear mother was my comfort and support. By the advice of my father, I went to Sevier County and took up a quarter section of land. I went to St. George at the completion of the Temple, and met many dear friends and relatives; my father was there, and those who were present, will, I believe, never forget the heavenly intercourse enjoyed by the Saints while thus convened. Shortly after our return to the city, our honored father was stricken down with his last sickness. Never was there a more solemn scene than that witnessed at his death, his family were there, also the head men of the

Church. Physicians with their futile skill were standing round, the faith and anxiety of the whole Church were centered around that dying form and departing soul of God's Prophet at that trying hour. His body unconscious now to pain, was there before us, but his noble spirit already saw behind the veil which screens from us the immortal spheres. 'Joseph! Joseph!' were his last words, and when he breathed his last his face became radient as if molten sunbeams had been poured into his veins, giving him an unearthly and celestial appearance never to be forgotten by those who surrounded his dying couch. After a settlement of our father's estate I removed to Provo in order to give my dear children and myself the advantages of attending the Brigham Young Academy. In January of this same year, President Taylor sent me, in company with Sister Emmeline B. Wells, to visit the Woman's Suffrage Convention held in Washington. After my return I began teaching in the Brigham Young Academy, taking charge of the young ladies and organizing a work class; also the primary department in which position I have been actively engaged ever since. The Brigham Young Academy was endowed by inspiration by him whose name it bears. Professor Karl G. Maeser was called to act as principal at the commencement, and when he asked for instruction from its noble founder, he received only this: 'Ask God to guide you in all things and carry it on under His directions; this is all I have to say.'

"From that time Professor Maeser has faithfully lived to fulfill the wishes of its founder. How he has succeeded is demonstrated every year by the hundreds of young men and women who there receive for the first time a knowledge and testimony of this Gospel. Too much praise cannot be bestowed upon the Honorable Board: President A. O. Smoot, Harvey Cluff, Wilson H. Dusenberry, Bishop Myron Tanner, Bishop Harrington, Bishop Bringhurst and Sister Coray for their energy and labor to make this school all that Brigham Young intended it should be.

"In the deeds bestowing a grant upon this institution it is plainly stated that the young men be taught mechanism, and the young ladies domestic duties. In accordance with this a young ladies' department has been organized and we have endeavored to carry out this peculiar feature desired by President Young, my beloved father.

"I have occupied the position of advisor and director to the young ladies for the past four years. I have now the advantage of a fine large room built expressly for this branch of education. Was called to preside over the Primary Associations of Provo, am a Counselor to the President of the Young Ladies' Mutual Improvement Association also; and an officer in the Provo Silk Association."

While living in Salt Lake City, Mrs. Zina Y. Williams was one of the committee superintending the decoration of the great Tabernacle. Large classes were taught artificial flower making, and thousands of yards of festoons and hanging baskets, interspersed with appropriate mottoes and flags made the vast ceiling a bower of beauty for many months. She has taught decorative work of different kinds in several towns of our Territory, possessing a special gift in this direction.

An energetic spiritual laborer, a loving daughter and faithful wife and mother, she has also a wide circle of sincere friends. She was the first of President Young's daughters to manifest prominently in the face of opposition, her willingness to unite with the associations organized for the repression of extravagance in dress, table expenditure and frivolity, and for the cultivation of spiritual knowledge, and mutual improvement. These meetings were regarded with aversion and even ridicule, by many, as tending to bring women into too great publicity. This proved to be an incorrect idea. Sister Willlams was one of the earliest spiritual laborers and has never faltered or deviated from her line of duty. President Young has other daughters also, who have later become officers and actively interested in the Women's Organizations among this people; and they will without doubt, develop many of those abilities, which, combined and made subservient to the will of God made the name of Brigham Young immortal in history.

LOUISE M. WELLS,

SECRETARY OF CENTRAL ORGANIZATION OF THE YOUNG LADIES'
MUTUAL IMPROVEMENT ASSOCIATIONS.

The fact that most of the ladies of this work are of mature,
and some even advanced years, suggests the thought—what
of the "rising generation" of this people? How have the
practical workings of this system which the world can judge
of only from report and occasional glimpses into its operations,
but which with the youth of the people is a literal and sole
experience—affected their ideas and purposes?

Time, steadfast determination and spiritual progress have
adjusted all mingled and varied elements of individualities
and nationalities in those who received the Gospel in scattered
homes in different parts of the earth, have overcome those
obstacles (which were such through inexperience in newly restored truths and laws,) and brought all to the proper level of
their individual sphere of action and usefulness. What a
piece of master-work has this been! Order out of confusion,
brotherhood created between stranger races.

It has been often said, "that when the old stock dies out, "
the world can better judge the worth of our doctrines; if they
survive and grow in the hearts of the succeeding generation
their parents did not plant the spiritual tree in lack of wisdom,
and it will after this test of years prove worthy of the serious
consideration of those who now deem it beneath their thoughtful attention.

More than fifty years have passed since the glorious message
was first proclaimed to the world; many of those true, noble
Saints who toiled as builder's of their Master's Kingdom have
finished their work, and with years filled with honors have

passed on to their rest and reward. A few years more, and the witnesses who lived in the days of Joseph and Hyrum will be gone, we shall be left to ourselves, their record and our God. Who will replace them? Are their posterity following in their footsteps? Yes, beneath the seeming swift current of youthtime's careless indifference runs an undercurrent of earnestness, integrity and—yes—royalty of soul. There can be found many of our young people who bear the impress of their destiny in their daily lives, their numbers are increasing, their works assuming prominence and recognition.

In connection with the young people's organizations it is due to Miss Louise M. Wells, that a brief record of her history and position form part of this work.

This young lady was born in Salt Lake City, August 27, 1862. On both her father and mother's side she is descended from families of the old Puritan stock. General Wells' record in Church history is one that earth's greatest men might be proud to possess, and he has received such a tribute of respect and love from our people as has rarely been recorded. Her mother is the editor of the *Woman's Exponent*, but has during her lifetime written constantly, amounting indeed to many volumes were her writings published; and is exceptionally gifted as a poetic writer. With such parents it may be reasonably expected that with her inherent endowments trained in the influence of the Gospel, with a fine spiritual nature, conscientious principles, an amiable disposition and quiet, gentle manner, Miss Wells will do credit to her parents and her people.

Of Louie, as she is familiarly called, it is said that when she was very young she gave evidence of musical talent by rendering in an original style, plaintive melodies admirably suited to her voice, and rich in that pathos that always touches the heart. With many, singing is an acquired accomplishment, with her it is as natural as to the nightingale. Also in her childhood she unconsciously disclosed artistic taste by gathering the autumn tinted leaves and grasses from the garden, which she arranged in quaint and pretty devices for home adornments. This talent was later cultivated under competent teachers, when she soon became qualified to give lessons privately and in classes, in drawing and painting. Already artists of distinction have pronounced her oil paintings of sufficient merit to entitle her to enter the Academy of Design in New York, and she has been advised to adopt art as a life vocation. On the occasion of the Church Jubilee, on Pioneer Day, 1880, Miss Wells was selected by the committee to represent Art. In 1882, in company with some of her relatives, she visited California, and there for the first time saw the ocean, one of nature's grandest pictures. During this visit she went through the art galleries of San Francisco. In 1883, she with her sister, Mrs. Sears, made a trip to the Eastern States, and visited the art galleries and museums of St. Louis, Chicago, Cleveland, New York, Boston, Philadelphia and Washington. Also had the opportunity of attending the World's Exposition at Boston. While visiting in the East she attended a reunion of the Dickinson's held at Amherst, Massachusetts, as a representative of the name, from whom her father descend ed through his grandmother, Experience Dickinson. Arriving at College Hall, where the reunion was celebrated, she met many hundreds of her kindred. Of this family I quote: " It is now almost two hundred and fifty years since Nathaniel Dickinson landed at Boston, and prior to 1634 found a home at Wethersfield, forty or fifty miles below Amherst. In 1659 he planted the permanent seat of our family, and deeply rooted the name of Dickinson, and here nine succeeding generations have risen to call him blessed. Nathaniel Dickinson died at Hadley, June 16, 1676. No pencil or artist has preserved to us the semblance of his features, no gravestone marks his resting-place. We only know that he sleeps in the only burying-ground at Hadley. "

At this reunion, which was quite an elaborate affair, a congratulatory letter was read from her father, General D. H. Wells, which elicited considerable applause, and the President, who had seen the General when visiting Salt Lake City, spoke of him in the highest terms.

Miss Wells was very cordially received by the hundreds of Dickinson's and succeeded in getting the names of many of the relatives of the family who are now sleeping in the old graveyard at Hadley, and from a "roll of honor" which hung upon the wall in the hall where the meeting was held, on which were inscribed the names of those who had made themselves distinguished. It was singular that this great meeting of the Dickinson's should have convened at the time when Miss Louie was visiting her mother's relatives only a few miles from Amherst, giving her an opportunity of meeting her father's kindred.

Louie visited Nauvoo, also Kirtland, where she went through the Temple. She has also proved herself to be a most charming press correspondent, by contributions to the *Exponent* that touched the heart of every Saint; letters that were as beautiful, fresh and sweet as spring-time. She has been connected with the *Exponent* for some time; is a writer for the *Contributor*, has been a member of the Tabernacle Choir for several years, and taught a department of Miss Cook's school in 1880 and 1881.

In June, 1880, Miss Wells was appointed Secretary to the Central Organization of the Young Ladies' Mutual Improvement Associations, Mrs. Elmina S. Taylor, President, a position of honor and importance, and which she fulfils with dignity and ability. As a Latter-day Saint, the young lady is worthy of her position and the love and confidence of her friends; and we look forward to her future with happy anticipations of beautiful works from her spirit and hand.

As in this work are represented the venerable silver-haired matrons, and the younger wife and mother, it seems beautifully appropriate that Miss Louie, in her youth and purity, should represent the daughters of Israel, looking towards the future with eyes of faith and confidence.

Explanatory of the Picture

REPRESENTATIVE WOMEN OF DESERET.

The first portrait in the first group of the picture, is that of ELIZA R. SNOW SMITH, President of the Latter-Day Saints' Women's Organizations. The second, on the left-hand side of the same group, ZINA D. H. YOUNG, First Counselor. Third, on the right-hand side, MARY ISABELLA HORNE, Treasurer. Fourth, SARAH M. KIMBALL, Secretary.

The above are the Presiding Board over all the Latter-Day Saints Women's Organizations.

At the head of the "Association Group" is, first, ELMINA S. TAYLOR, President of the Young Ladies' Mutual Improvement Associations. Second, MARY A. FREEZE, President of the Young Ladies Mutual Improvement Association of the Salt Lake Stake of Zion. Third, left-hand side, is LOUIE FELT, President of the Primary Associations. Fourth, ELLEN C. CLAWSON, President of the Primary Associations of the Salt Lake Stake of Zion.

At the head of the picture, left-hand corner, PHŒBE W. WOODRUFF, wife of President Wilford Woodruff. At the right-hand corner, BATHSHEBA W. SMITH, wife of President George A. Smith. At the left-hand corner, PRESCENDIA L. KIMBALL, a veteran Saint and pioneer. At the right-hand lower corner, ELIZABETH HOWARD, Secretary of the Relief Society of the Salt Lake Stake of Zion.

At the head of the fourth group is, EMMELINE B. WELLS, editor of *Woman's Exponent*. At the right-hand, same group, is ROMANIA B. PRATT, M. D.

Turning now to the four ladies on the left-hand side of the picture, the first is EMILY HILL WOODMANSEE, poet. Second, right-hand side, HANNAH T. KING, poet and prose author. Third, on the left, AUGUSTA JOYCE CROCHERON, author, and Secretary of the Young Ladies' Mutual Improvement Association of the Salt Lake Stake of Zion. Fourth, HELEN MAR WHITNEY, daughter of Heber C. Kimball, and writer of Church history and biographies; also First Counselor of the Relief Society of the Salt Lake Stake of Zion.

Returning to the fourth group: third portrait on the left, ZINA Y. WILLIAMS, daughter of Brigham Young, and President of the Primary Associations of the Utah Stake of Zion. Fourth, is LOUIE M. WELLS, daughter of President D. H. Wells; Secretary of Central Organizations of the Young Ladies' Mutual Improvement Associations. Vocalist and artist.

FINIS.